Monica C

# TO HAVE NOT, TO HOLD

© 2023 **Europe Books**| London
www.europebooks.co.uk | info@europebooks.co.uk

ISBN 9791220141666
First edition: July 2023

**TO HAVE NOT, TO HOLD**

*I dedicate this book to my children, Darroll and Celeste, who endured long hours without my attention whilst I burnt the midnight oil.*

*Monica.*

# Chapter 1

She knows without a doubt that she is leaving.

This morning she can see it clearly, as clearly as the daylight streaming through the curtain onto him where he lies snoring next to her, alcoholic stink contaminating the room.

During the night the fears seem to have dropped down to the bottom of the list where they belong. Money, place to stay, what to say to the family. This morning they seem unimportant, for she knows that she is leaving him.

But by next week you will know that she didn't leave. Can you believe it? She still doesn't leave.

By the time she had gone about her work that day and come home, life had turned the list upside down once again and the fact that he had beaten her up again the night before went to the bottom of the list, and she swept aside the most important reason why she should leave the man.

Again, it was another morning.

She gasped for air as she surfaced from the underwater of sleep. A bang on the front door had awoken her. Confused, she glanced at the bedside clock. 30 Minutes after midnight.

Jeanie clutched her belly, holding the slightly sagging folds between her fingers. A habit of many years gone, and many to come. She swung her legs off the bed and sat quietly for a moment, trying to focus her mind.

Still grasping her tummy, she stood up, trying with all her will to connect her mind through her hand to awaken her ovaries as they lay dead inside her, trying mentally to force them to release just one egg – to connect with the sperm still warm and eager inside her from their love-making just ten minutes before.

'Please let it happen – just this once,' she prayed as she reached for her dressing gown. After seven long, hopeful years of marriage, still a futile wish. For her, who held and loved other women's babies each day, the desire for a baby of her own might always be only a wish.

The next loud knock, impatient, panicky and fast, woke him up. 'Shall I tell them you're out on a call? Then Smith can take this one,' Gregory murmured, trying to be nice. How she disliked him when he was being nice. She breathed disgust onto the back of his head as he turned the other way.

'Ok, hold on, don't break the door down!' she called to the door banger as she put on her slippers, trying to pat into place a thick mop of virgin African hair, as she ran down the passage to the front door.

The boy who stood there looked more tired than she felt, his chest heaving from running.

'Nurse Dean?' his voice squeaked in constricted adolescence.

'Yes. Come inside,' she said breathlessly, as a gust of wind blew rain into her face.

As she struggled to close the door against the wind his words rushed out over a slight lisp. 'My sister is going to have a baby any minute. Will you please come quickly?'

She turned to him, water dripping from his tattered overalls onto her immaculate beige carpet.

'What's her name, where does she live?' praying quietly that it was not on the outskirts of Elsies River.

'On the other side of the railway line'. That was about 5 kilometres away.

'How did you get here? Why could you not have phoned? You have my telephone number at home, haven't you?'

She knew instantly by his confused look that this was one of those. He wet his lips and looked down. No answer.

'Well – what is her name?'

'Mary.'

'Then why could you not use the telephone?' A senseless question. She already knew the answer.

'We don't have a phone. Nobody has a phone where we live.' This godforgotten Cape Town township, she cursed, staring at him impatiently, as if it was his fault that there was just one public telephone in the whole area. It was, after all, Cape Town in the mid-seventies. Probably vandalised, anyway.

Then she remembered: 'I don't, definitely not, have any patients on my list from your side of the railway line.'

Again, the eyes dropped. Silence. Definitely one of those unbooked cases again! Oh Lord. Her heart sank. This sounded like trouble. The woman could have all sorts of complications: kidney trouble, weak heart, diabetes. And to get a doctor out at night into the slums of Elsies River was impossible.

She could tell him to go away. Nobody would know. And, anyway, nobody would take notice of a sad-looking character like this one complaining that the nurse would not come when the woman's name was not on any clinic list.

She met his eyes again and the sadness of her people, for her people, pricked at the back of her eyes as she caught his look of helplessness. Her impatience turned to guilt, for her privileged position gave her no rights that everybody else does not have, no matter how illiterate or poor they might be. It was not until much later that she was to realise exactly how poor.

'How old is she and how many babies has she had?"

'Kanalla nurse,' (please nurse) 'Can't we first go and then I'll answer your questions?' he said respectfully, sensibly.

What was the use, though. Better get it over with quickly she thought, her irritation subsiding. 'Wait here while I get ready.' No sense in questioning him any further, though it would have helped to know when the pains had started and how many minutes between contractions. But then what would he know, anyway. He was just a lad.

There was no time to pause and be afraid to go in the car with an unknown young man. Or to even think that she might be letting herself in for trouble driving into a shantytown with no decent street lighting and hardly any roads. Or that she might have the car door ripped open at any street corner.

The district midwife's nightmare.

'Please lock your door when you get in,' she said as they walked to the car. He got into the front passenger seat sheepishly and sat leaning forward almost against the instrument panel, trying to sit lightly so no dirt from his overalls stayed behind.

No response to the turn of the key. She tried again. No response.

Suddenly the boy next to her became a man. A man who knew what to do and how to do it. 'Nothing serious, nurse, sounds like the battery terminal's lose. I'll tighten it for you.' And before she knew what was happening, he was out in front of the car signing for her to open the bonnet.

'Where are your spanners?' his voice drifted an octave higher on the wind. She reached over and lifted the back seat of the state-supplied Anglia and handed him the little brown paper packet which she called her tools, while pulling the lever down to open the bonnet.

'Ok, start it now,' from behind the lid. The engine sprang into life and purred.

He got back into the car with a different body, the small achievement pulling his back straight. He gave her a confident smile.

Jeanie turned to the business of driving with self-reproach. What one sees is what one wants to see. A hardworking, capable young man was briefly finding himself out of his depth. A man who could be trusted and was eager to help, unlike the pathetic somebody I'm stuck with in matrimony, she thought as she crunched the gears embarrassingly.

By this time the rain was really pelting down and it took some careful driving not to skid in the muddy streets. But perhaps now she could get some idea of what she was heading for. 'How old is Mary?' 'Sixteen.' Quietly.

'First time?'

'Yes.' It sounded like the night was going to be a long one. She drove along in silence for a few minutes. He sat hunched up in the seat next to her, hands pinched between his legs, frowning into the night.

Somewhere, deep inside her, the feeling started up again, the unstoppable wave of jealousy and frustration, breaking out of the barren depths of her infertile womb. Again, unconsciously, she put her left hand over her abdomen, wondering why life is so unfair. Why deny me the same right readily given to a young girl, who probably did not even want the baby?

Then years of discipline and experience came to her rescue as she glanced at the young man next to her. She swung her mind back to her job, knowing that it would, as always, help her to forget.

'When did it start?' she asked after a while, trying to hide the pain from her voice.

'Dunno,' he murmured to the windscreen. 'I came home from my friend's place, and she was screaming. They told me to fetch you.' 'And you ran all the way to my house?' 'Ya,' as if that were not important.

'You are cold,' she realised, seeing him shiver. 'Would you like to reach over onto the back seat and cover yourself with the blanket?' 'It's alright. Don't worry 'bout me, nurse. Sorry to worry you.' 'Is your sister married?' She knew the answer.

'No.' Obviously she would get no more out of him.

'Please lock your door,' she said after a while when she saw he had not done so. He locked the door without question. Both of them knew that they had to stop at the red traffic light ahead and there was no knowing what dangers lurked there. She dropped her speed, hoping the light would change to amber before she got to the crossroad and when it did, she put her foot down and charged across without stopping.

'Turn here,' he said while peering intently through the windscreen, eyes screwed up to see through the pelting rain. 'Turn right, then park up by the bridge at the end of this street,' he said, about 500 metres along.

She parked, locked up and followed him. They crossed over the rickety, narrow, wooden bridge to the other side of the railway line into darkness.

No streetlights at all now, for they were entering proper shantytown. Mud and dirt everywhere. It reminded Jeanie about overhearing a little white boy asking his dad in the first-class carriage on the train the other day why do they like to live like that, in the dark, everything is grey, no lights - as if some people ask to be placed in darkness.

But there were no more houses when they reached the end of the street. Was he lost?

'Stop here,' he mumbled, 'the house is over there,' pointing. Through the darkness her eye caught a lump of rubble about ten metres ahead. He kept his eyes down, in embarrassment.

The large, galvanized sheet lying diagonally suspended over a corrugated zinc wall used to be a vertical shack before the wind rent it down around their lives.

He continued to walk through mud and rubble. The shrieking wind attacked their ears, carrying a scream of pain on its back.

Jeanie had to be very careful where she put her feet, for there was water everywhere. The entrance to what her companion had optimistically called 'the house' was miraculously pushed aside by him without falling down.

He simply bent down and lifted a bit of the corrugated iron sheeting, politely waiting for her to crouch in ahead of him. She ducked and crouched forward as if entering a two-person tent.

They had obviously been hard at work these past twenty-four hours to secure what was left of their home. The rear zinc iron walls were still standing, although the one on the right was leaning over threateningly. On this side of the curtain suspended across the room stood a lone table in the middle of the section which served as a kitchen/sitting room.

A weather-beaten, overweight middle-aged woman struggled to lift her body from the low, drab settee. But her face was kind, and it creased into a smile without front teeth.

'Thank you for coming, nurse. I've got the water boiling and managed to get some old newspapers from the shop before they closed.'

On the other side of the curtain with its red and orange floral pattern Jeanie saw the young girl, her face contorted, as a steely contraction attacked her. She was screaming into her left palm, while trying to apply pressure to her bulging belly to lessen the pain with the other hand. She was half-lying on some blankets on the floor, supported by pillows against the wall.

Opposite her and against the other less sturdy wall was a small bed on which lay a very old woman, her sad eyes staring up at the nurse. No introductions or niceties here. Poverty and pain are a couple which, when travelling together like treacherous twins, leave space for only emptiness and raw emotion.

'Ouma can't get up, she's had a stroke,' the woman said apologetically.

'Good evening, Ouma,' Jeanie greeted the old lady as is the custom, with the respect she would give to her own grandmother.

'Would you be able to work on the floor? Sorry, nurse. Sorry for the trouble,' the mother said, shyly, with downcast eyes.

Jeanie's concern was for the young girl. She reached out her hand and the girl grasped it, her nails digging into the nurse's palm as another contraction folded her body and arched her back like a tightly pulled bow about to eject its arrow into the cruel night.

'Hello, Mary. I'm Jeanie Dean,' she said when the girl opened her eyes as the contraction receded. 'Everything will be all right. Do you think you could move down a bit and open your legs while I feel what the baby is up to?'

It took Mary a minute to drag her mind away from her pain. Shaking her head, she blinked her eyes, partly to get rid of the tears filling her lower lids and also to give herself a brief moment to drift away with the receding pain.

Then she slowly let go of the nurse's hand and hooked in her elbows to shift herself down.

The nurse opened her bag and put on her surgical gloves, timing the next contraction. None for at least thirty seconds. Not too serious, she thought.

And as she gently separated Mary's legs and sat on her haunches to insert her fingers into the vagina to feel how dilated the cervix was, a subtle change occurred.

The nurse was no longer the privileged, educated professional surrounded by a myth of knowledge and importance. Now she was merely a woman, faced with another woman in pain. And neither of them need be pregnant nor give birth for the two of them to be women together.

The seriousness of birth hung over their heads and the acrid smell of birth fluid rising into Jeanie's nostrils from the nearness of the girl brought them closer together. Both of them knew the magnitude of the task at hand, that their joint strength was required to get through it.

More than four fingers dilated. And another contraction coming.

'Mary,' the nurse almost whispered, so as not to let her become hysterical, 'try to breathe in deeply as the pain gets worse. I know you feel like bearing down but please, let's get baby to slip down as far as it will go before you push to get it out. Ok?' A nod.

No antenatal training here. No good lessons about breathing or relaxation. No idea about the dangerous situation she might be in. Just the quiet knowledge that she was being looked after. Relief that someone had come to help.

Like a woman who had carefully planned this for months ahead and who had been through all of this before, Mary took a deep breath, put her hands on the floor beside her and breathed out slowly as yet another contraction turned her belly into a hard ball. Her mother took a cloth and wiped her forehead.

Prima gravida. First pregnancy. And first birth, which means that the whole female physiology was being tested for the first time. And there was no knowing how things might turn out. Nurse Dean knew that all her training and experience were being tested in this delivery. She watched the girl carefully.

As another contraction hit Mary, the girl gasped and gave a loud scream.

'Try to relax, Mary,' as the girl put her legs down and tried to roll over onto her side, not knowing how to get rid of the pain. The casual conversations Mary might have had with her friends about birth had not prepared her for the severity of labour. The shock on her face showed that the pain, scorching viciously deep inside her like a red-hot iron, had not been expected.

Mary's mother was kneeling on the other side, gently rubbing the girl's back. Then Mary whipped around, pulling her knees hard up against a taut abdomen, closing her mouth to suppress another scream.

Gently, the nurse pushed the girl onto her back, almost pleading with her. 'I know this will be very hard for you, Mary,' she said, 'but could you try to breathe in deeply when you feel the pain coming? That will give me a

chance to see whether the baby is ready to be born. When
_'

Before she could finish, Mary's face turned red as she held her breath, the veins in her neck and on her temples and forehead standing out with pressure. A long, muffled groan escaped through her clenched teeth as she pushed down with all her might.

'Please open your legs,' the nurse said, realising that it would be very difficult to stop her now, wanting to see whether the baby's head had shifted down far enough through the pelvic cavity for it to be born.

It was all over within ten minutes. First came the crown of the little black head, then the upturned, wrinkled, pink face. But for a slight tear, Mary gave birth, quickly and cleanly, to a little girl.

Seeing the world upside down for the first time, the baby screamed. And the women laughed their relief as Mary shyly smiled a quiet 'thank you' up to the nurse.

With a concentration close to reverence Jeanie tied the umbilical cord tightly with surgical gut in two places close to each other, not far from the baby's tummy. Then she carefully cut between the ties, separating mother and baby physically, praying that their emotional and spiritual cord would remain strong.

'What do you want to do with the afterbirth?' she asked, looking down and speaking directly to the eldest of the four female generations in the room.

The old lady's eyes lit up with the gratitude of illness and age for being consulted. She smiled lopsidedly over her pillow which was wet with dribbled saliva, nodded her head then quickly shook it in cerebral confusion, trying to project wisdom from her half world.

Jeanie thought she knew what the old lady was trying to say. As did this family, Jeanie came from mixed Malaysian ancestry, where the placenta is believed to be the twin of the baby, and has its own spirit, which has to be respected.

But she also knew about the commercial use of "placenta extract" found in some cosmetics, such as facial cream sold in France. At that time placentas were still being collected in hospitals without the knowledge or permission of mothers, bought and shipped to France to be used by pharmaceutical firms. The people suspected that this was being done, but never had any proof.

'We will bury the afterbirth, nurse,' said the mother from her knees, cleaning up the floor around the now sleeping Mary.

And that is how it was done that day.

How then could Nurse Dean refuse the offer of a cup of coffee out of a caffeine-stained, cracked mug? The eagerness of the offer, warmth of feeling and strong blackness of the coffee wiped out any thought of health risks or attitude.

There were no recriminations between mother and daughter. That might happen later. The future seemed far away, the future with its problems of rearing a child in their situation. But the future did not exist in those ten minutes while Jeanie sat on the little bed, next to the old lady, watching the mother fussing about cleaning.

'No, don't move, nurse, you've done enough. Thank God you came.'

Thank God, too, that I'd had no time to check blood pressure before, or test urine or look for oedema, for I probably would have been shocked, the nurse thought, nodding quietly at the woman as she checked Mary's blood pressure.

'You will need to get her to a doctor to get the blood pressure down a bit,' she warned them, but knew that without money or transport, this might never happen.

Jeanie lifted her bag and was about to leave when she hesitantly said, 'Mrs. Wallace?'

The woman looked up at her expectantly, eager to please. 'Yes, nurse?'

Jeanie could not meet the woman's eyes. Mary had gone to sleep and so, it seemed, had the grandmother, whose eyes were closed too.

Looking down at her hands, Jeanie bent forward and said quietly so that only the mother could hear, 'Has Mary, ...er, have you, thought of putting the baby up for adoption?' ending with a quick intake of breath, holding it anxiously as she now looked up and met the woman's kindly eyes.

'Adoption?' The shock on the woman's face at the mere thought of such a suggestion banished all the nurse's hopes. 'No way, nurse.' Emphatically. And after a brief pause, not knowing she was shattering Jeanie's hopes, she continued, 'She's made her bed. She's got to sleep on it,' with finality.

Jeanie merely sighed and, after a hurried 'Good luck, we'll send someone around later today,' she left.

'I'll walk you back to the car, nurse,' he said from the dark somewhere outside the entrance, and she jumped. She turned and he reached for her bag, walking away from the house with her.

Jeanie could not believe that the young man had been standing under the overhang outside the front entrance all that time, waiting for her to come out. Her respect for him increased.

She nodded and smiled, suddenly now less tired and satisfied, as she fell in step with him. He saw her safely over the bridge to her car. Before he left her, he reminded her to keep the doors locked.

The rain had let up and had turned into a slight drizzle and she could see clearly through the rear window. The Cape Town south easterly wind had disappeared as dramatically as it had started. The morning was going to be one of the unexpected soft ones, which only temperamental, Mediterranean Cape Town could promise.

She drove over the big railway bridge, where suddenly the streets were well lit, with deserted pavements. A police car crawled past from the other side, the driver staring suspiciously at her.

Of course. It was South Africa in the seventies, and she was passing through the white side of town. The police would make sure of their people's security.

The houses were discreetly lit over well-kept lawns, blue waters of the occasional swimming pool peeping through upright fences under security lights. Like the owners behind their walls, the houses stood white, stiff, upright and conservative. She heard fear in the bark of a big dog from behind the fence of the house at the next street corner.

And as she negotiated the turns, she felt the pride which Capetonians feel when their heads are above the mess of Apartheid, and they gain strength from the mountains all around them.

She felt peaceful and fulfilled.

By this time, she was back on the deserted streets of her section of town.

She did not notice that two cars were behind her, then joined by a third. They made no effort to overtake her, even though she was driving along very slowly.

Jeanie was to arrive home thirty-six hours later.

## Chapter 2

It was well after sunset when Jeanie drove into her driveway at home the next evening.

When she had left, Gregory had been asleep. Now – what will she find? She felt afraid of the argument which inevitably lay ahead. His temper flared up so easily.

Suspicious as he was, it would be almost impossible to explain where she had been without being in touch. That is, if he gave her a chance to explain, for she knew that he did not usually allow her any say when he had made up his mind that she needed to be 'taught a lesson'.

She carefully parked her car next to her husband's green Volvo. Before getting out of the car, her eyes closed in a brief prayer.

She felt soiled and exhausted.

They had released her only about half an hour before. They had kept her locked up and alone in the little room for hours and hours on end, except when they came in two, once even three of them, to question her.

Gregory would want some answers. She knew her husband well. His endless suspicions about her, his inability to even consider her political commitment.

She knew it would be hard to explain to him that she had not wanted to make him worry about her and that not coming home had not been her fault. But at best of times, it was almost impossible to communicate with him. She knew that he would not give her time to explain before he exploded.

'Please God, let him be sober,' she prayed, eyes still closed, weariness now flooding her. She shivered from fear and exhaustion. The emasculation of interrogation lingered in her psyche, making her feel weak. Her dry tongue was furred with a bitter taste of hatred and lack of sleep.

Half expecting Gregory to come storming out of the house, she slowly came to life. Not to disturb him, she closed the car door very quietly and walked stealthily to the front door.

The shadow which her slender body cast against the side wall of the impressive detached house looked disjointed. Her thick hair looked exaggerated and extended, an early moon throwing ghastly shapes of her flattish nose and soft, round lips across the curve of the wall.

'The windows of the world are covered with rain…' Isaac Hayes sang through the open window. The words of the song increased her melancholy and fear. The stereo was loud. His favourite song, at his favourite volume, when drunk.

She clumsily struggled to unlock the front door with her right hand, while holding her nurse's cloak and black bag in the other.

She went straight to the stereo in the far corner of the sitting room, cutting off the sound and '…where is the sunshine we once knew?' trailed into silence. Like the words, the sunshine had disappeared from their lives.

The Gregory she had married was no longer around. During the early days of their marriage Jeanie had thought that there was no more exciting, intelligent and nice man alive, but the attraction had disappeared all too quickly.

Jeanie rushed into the bathroom and locked the door, believing her husband to be asleep. First things first.

Not wanting to wake Gregory up, she ran just enough water into the bath to wash herself down quickly, without removing her uniform.

As she came out of the bathroom he appeared from the passage. He looked a mess. His usually immaculate trousers were creased. He tried to close the zip while looking at her with his head slightly tilted to the right, like a kitten intrigued by a moving object.

With contradiction, Jeanie felt a fleeting endearment, as he raised his right arm to wipe the sleep from his eyes, like an infant, scratching at his ribs with his left hand before waking up completely, at the same time trying to lick the dryness of sleep and the dehydration of alcohol from his parched lips.

But all endearments flew from her head with his 'Where the fuck have you been!' as soon as his consciousness arrived.

Determined to keep the conversation factual for as long as possible, she said 'Hello Greg. Like a cup of coffee?'

He looked at her for a moment, his upper lip pulled across even teeth. 'Don't waste time, Jeanie, I asked you a question,' he said through thin lips.

'Greg, do you mind sitting down to have a chat?' she asked, knowing that the time of truth had arrived.

'Better be good,' he said. But instead of sitting down, he disappeared into the kitchen and came back with a can of beer in his hand.

To talk sense to someone who was still half drunk from the last bout of drinking, and starting to drink again, would take quite a bit of self-control.

She sat down on an armchair in the lounge, her back to the front door. Her heart started to beat rapidly. She hoped that Gregory was not past the point of reason, as he became when he had drunk too much.

He opened the can of beer and took a long swig before he sat down on the easy chair opposite her.

'So?'

She wanted to tell him about the police, but the fear was rising up in her like a hot flush. To have time to think, she started to explain.

'When I left from the house I was at – at about half past two on Tuesday night – er – Wednesday morning, when I got to the corner of 15th Avenue and Halt Road, a car drove in front of me while another pulled next to me. They forced me to stop. I did, and…' All true so far, except that she was given no chance to continue, with truth or without.

'You with your eternal lies!' he almost shouted.

'I'm not telling lies,' her frightened little-girl voice had arrived.

'Can't you make up a better story? You expect me to believe that? Were you raped or something? And if you were, how come you're sitting there looking so smug? Enjoy it, did ya?'

She shut up. He was not going to listen to any of her problems. This is why she had stopped communicating anything but the most superficial part of her life to him ages ago.

'This is what angers me about you,' he said through pursed lips, now waving his half-drunk can of beer around, white foam running over its sides. 'Why do you have to make as if your life is so dramatic when we all know that you've been w'oring around again?'

'What do you mean, that I'm being dramatic?' Fear made her voice go squeaky, like a mouse waiting to be snatched. 'You asked me where I was and I'm trying to tell you, so give me a chance.' Jeanie could see all the signs: eyes staring fixedly, pulsation on temple, lips tightening up in temper.

'Shut up! I really hate your superiority. Who do you think you're talking to?' he shouted.

She just stared at him. No matter what she said, her answer would be the wrong one.

He jumped up, threw his empty beer can against the wall, brown foam staining her hair along the way. She cowered forward, arms covering her head, knowing that he was going for her face.

He grabbed her by the hair and pulled her upright, to face him. She was paralyzed. Why does fear have such a debilitating effect on me, she wondered wildly while he gave her a severe shake and a push, so her head jerked back, almost hitting the wall behind her. Then he slapped her hard across her right cheek.

She screamed as the force of the blow threw her back into the chair. She stayed there, covering her face with her hands, expecting him to lose control completely.

She waited for the rest of the attack, which did not come. Instead, she felt his heavy breath on the outside of her hands, and slowly opened her eyes.

Gregory had somehow got hold of a broomstick, which he'd jammed across her legs and was holding down with arms wide spread, bending forward over it, until his Roman nose almost touched hers.

Her neck pulled back stiffly, she stared at him, mesmerized by the dark brown eyes staring fixedly at her like an eagle spotting its prey.

'You're fucking around. I know. If that's the game you want to play, then fuck off and go and do it in the street, where you belong, you-', beer soaked spittle and fumes spitting into her face.

For a moment they faced each other – like two dogs, motionless in mid-fight, tensely waiting for a move from the other.

With a grunt through clenched teeth, Gregory gave the broomstick a push against Jeanie's stomach and lifted it abruptly with disgust above his head. The broomstick went flying across the room.

She ducked as he reached for the doorknob just past her head, thinking that he was going to strike her again. Instead, he opened the door, stormed out and banged it shut behind him.

She sat there until she felt cramps in her calves. Motionless and quiet, defenceless and listless, she sat there, her mind in turmoil, her dry eyes staring at the opposite wall while the shadows of night crept into the room. Her pain was more than physical. She felt drained and mindless. She felt like the half-woman Gregory was always accusing her of being.

All because she had been unable to bear him a child.

## Chapter 3

Too tired to do anything else, Jeanie eventually dragged herself through the passage into the bedroom, dejected, not bothering to switch on any lights or lock the doors, not knowing what time it was. Her coat and bag were lying where they had landed hours before, in the middle of the floor, but she had not the energy to bend down to pick them up.

Everything had gone quiet as she kicked off her shoes. She just about remembered to slip on a pair of clean knickers before she fell across the big bed.

When she awoke after a light, brief sleep, the room was in complete darkness. The pains in her stomach failed to remind her that she had not eaten for more than a day. The stomach has its own way of reacting violently to violence, she thought, as she sat up on the bed and took her uniform off. She did not bother to take off anything else, and wearily moved around until she had covered herself with the sheet and bed cover.

Sleep, however, would not come. She lay there in the dark, listening to every little noise the night made. Each car which passed set her nerves on edge. Her body was tense and stiff in anticipation of further harm.

In shock she watched her hand go to the ashtray on the bedside cabinet beside her. In slow motion, she watched herself lift it and throw it into Gregory's face as he stood in the doorway. And as he lunged towards her, she made a grab for the knife hidden under her pillow, holding it in a tight grip, straight into his descending chest.

With a whimper, her forehead wet with sweat, Jeanie surfaced from a nightmare. She sat bolt upright on the bed. My God! That could so easily have been real.

The sound of Gregory's car had awoken her.

She quickly lay down again, covered her head and closed her eyes. Every nerve in her body was tight and alert. She heard him open the front door and, without putting on any lights, walk down the passage towards the bedroom.

She expected her husband to be drunk and she could hardly breathe. She lay there, stiff and frightened.

He did not bother to switch the light on. She heard him fumbling about while he got undressed. Then he climbed into bed beside her. She felt the warmth of his naked body close to her.

He smelt of shame, contrition, and Old Spice. Sober.

Silence. He lit a cigarette and lay there in the dark, deep in his own thoughts. She opened her eyes slightly and watched the reflection of the burning ember at the tip of his fag moving in a semi-circle in the wardrobe mirror on her side of the bed. The glowing blob of fire hypnotized her, moving up and down each few seconds. Her body would not let go and she twitched her toes in an effort to relax.

'Cold?' he asked, feeling her shiver.

'Mm…no. I've just woken up,' she lied into the bed cover over her nose.

'Want to talk now?' he asked softly while purposely leaning over her to kill his cigarette in the ashtray on her side of the bed, forcing his body to make contact with hers.

'What's the use, Greg? I don't think we need go through it all again. I'm so tired.' She could say this only because she knew he was sober.

As she said it, she felt her man's need, sadly, pathetically. She realised that he had a deep need to be told that he was still ok. That he was still her man, that she recognised him as someone important in her life. She knew that he wanted to hear her say that there was no other man in her life. This would satisfy his ego.

She felt deep regret. She was unable to transmit her feelings, her understanding, to him. What could she say? That she still loved him? No. Instead, she decided to explain. 'Greg, I was busy all night. There was no phone where I could contact you from and, even if there was, I couldn't leave to make a call. It was an emergency.' All true, wasn't it?

'I don't know what I would do if I should lose you,' he almost cried into her neck as if he had not heard her. 'I'm sorry' – always sorry after the event, 'I'm sorry I hit you, Jeanie. I promise I won't do it again. It is just that sometimes I lose control and cannot stop myself. God, I hate myself for being such a beast when I really do love you so much'.

And she believed him. She believed him once again. She believed him in the incomprehensible, sick way she had been doing for seven years. Pity mixed with grief, grief with unbelief, unbelief with sadness.

Jeanie's heart started pounding at an entirely different rate. His vulnerability always affected her in the most extraordinary way. She did feel so sorry for this man who seemed utterly lost and directionless.

It was impossible for her to try to analyse her feelings towards Gregory. The fact was that, right now, she felt a compassion for him which made her chest go tight and hot tears of – of what? – she could not stop to consider – flooded her eyes.

She blinked her tears away in the dark and said, 'I just don't know, Greg. I don't know what makes us the way we are. I can't understand why we hurt each other so much. I'm confused,' taking blame where none was meant to rest.

He turned her face towards him and, realising that the tears were now quietly running down the side of her face onto his palm, he tenderly used the tips of his fingers to wipe them away.

'Please don't cry, my Jeanie. I promise it won't happen again.' But of course, it did.

She heard a dog bark into the now silent night and, not stopping to consider whether it was their common need for tenderness and understanding which was crying out for satisfaction or an untimely expression of love, Jeanie allowed herself to be enfolded in the arms of a man she, almost, hated.

## Chapter 4

Jeanie vaguely remembered Gregory's leg resting heavily over her during the night. She pushed it off, and turned abruptly on her side with her back to him. The bonus of sleep did not extend to forgiveness.

She woke with a start when he kissed her cheek as he came out of the bathroom. Her body went into its usual stiffness at an unexpected touch from him with his smell of soap and flatulence. She was to hate the smell of his aftershave for the rest of her life. Its repugnant fumes penetrated and muddled her cloudy thoughts.

'I'm off to Upington today, love, remember?' he said as he placed a cup of coffee beside her.

She said nothing, pretending still to be asleep. She had forgotten that he would be away for two days on an audit and her spirit lifted. The reminder woke her up and gave her cheeks the energy needed to put a smile on her face as she opened her eyes.

'O yeah. Forgot 'bout that. You'll be ok getting to the airport?' stretching, trying to keep the relief from her voice.

'Yes, I'll be all right. Salim is giving me a lift.' He pinched her cheek. 'Will you be ok?'

'Yeah. Think I'll take the day off, if I can get someone to stand in for me.'

'Enjoy yourself honey,' winking as he walked out of the bedroom, and her day brightened.

She jumped out of bed lightly and peeked through the curtain. The day looked warm and windless, the early morning sun smiling promisingly through far away, light blue clouds in front of Table Mountain, which she could see in the distance.

Then she inspected her face in the big mirror. No visible bruises, thank God. Her left eye felt slightly tender as she touched the lid. A few small blood vessels in the far corner had erupted but could not be seen, except when she turned her eye inward. Thank God the humiliation of the past two nights was not there for the world to see.

Dislike for Gregory sat in her throat like bile. No number of justifications or regrets from him could diffuse her humiliation.

She decided to do her nursing calls, not to take the day off. She could take the afternoon off and do the things which needed to be done.

Within the hour, her uniform lending her the outer respectability that her inner lacked, she drove into Matroosfontein.

She loved this little suburb with its red brick houses, row upon row of them, all looking the same. One of the few places where one could still see chimneys in use. She stood for a moment to enjoy the sight of smoke drifting lazily up from a few chimneys, spiralling lightly against the pale blue sky.

Jeanie was born in Matroosfontein, into the regimented lives of post-war working people. Here railway workers had been settled, most of them for the first time in their lives in their own little homes. Although her father had not been a railway worker, he had somehow been allowed to rent one of the sturdy houses from the local town council.

She walked the two streets from where her car was parked to the house she wanted to visit. She did not want her car to be seen outside the house.

Walking along, she thought of the happy days she had spent on the sand hills on the outskirts of the town, before they had built the big main road behind it.

There still were no pavements, and she had to jump out of the way of passing cars, getting splattered with mud.

'Hello Nurse Dean,' she heard many times. Many of them she recognised as patients, some children in school uniform whom she remembered having helped into the world, and older folk. She felt happy here, flattered by the attention and goodwill she received.

The little mongrel recognised her as she opened the wire gate of the house in 5th Street. It jumped around her legs making little coughing noises. 'What a hopeless guard dog you are!' she said as she bent down to give the dog a pat.

At that moment an old man came walking around the side of the house.

'Jeanie!' his face lit up with pleasure. She went to him and hugged him warmly, feeling his ribs through the thin shirt. His old, greasy, brown hat fell forward over his nose as he stepped back from her, holding his hands around her waist, taking in the vitality of her with delight.

'Long time no hear, Jeanie.' They spoke in their own tongue, the patoi Afrikaans spoken by the Cape Coloureds.

Apartheid classified the people of South Africa into five different groups. The most advantaged were those who carried identity documents marked White, after them the Coloureds and then the Indians (with decreasing educational and social advantages) and lastly, without decent housing, sanitation, health services or proper schooling, the most disadvantaged group, the ethnic Africans such as the Xhosas and Zulus. And the fifth group was Other. Hardly anyone knew what 'other' meant.

Jeanie and her family were classed as Coloured because they were not black skinned and came from a mixed ancestry of Khoikhoi, African, Dutch, British, Malaysian – and any of the many other explorers and sailors who had sailed past the tip of Africa and left their seed behind.

'Ya, oom (uncle) Daan' she said, laughing. 'How have you been? They been feeding you properly?'

'These youngsters are too busy to worry with an old man,' Oom Daan's light brown, weatherworn face creased into comfortable folds. He tried to laugh but the laugh turned into a deep-chested, gurgling cough and he had to bend forward as he tried to stop it.

Jeanie looked at him with concern. He could not stop coughing and she stood quietly, waiting for it to die down. He spat on the ground and looked up at her when it subsided, his teary old eyes red. 'It's been bad lately, Jeanie,' he said apologetically.

She felt a mixture of sorrow and anger. Oom Daan lived on whatever scraps he could collect from the neighbours. She knew that he had probably not had a decent meal for a while. His miserable state pension just about allowed him to pay his rent for his little room, to a landlord as poor as he.

The pride in his stiff back as he led the way to the back of the house warned her not to make any comments, and she remained silent.

'Look who I've got here,' he called through the locked door of the outside room, lightly knocking on the window next to the door.

A young black face peeped through the small window and the boy who opened the door was no more than 13 years old. His handsome face lit up into a broad grin showing sparkling, white, even teeth. Jeanie stepped into the single room and greeted him with a warm hug.

She shook hands with the man and woman who were there, in the style of old comrades, first a formal handshake with palms together, then, swinging the hand up in a half circle playfully gripping each other's thumbs.

'I was expecting you later, sister,' said the man, pulling her by the thumb into his broad chest. He was about her age, in his early thirties. He towered above her. His face and tattered shirt were covered with black ink from the old Gestetner duplicating machine which they were working on.

'Hi J,' said the woman and she went to turn the handle of the copying machine which looked as tired as she did.
'How's it been, all?'

'Ok,' Joe said. 'we're all ready for you. How many do you think you can get rid of?' He walked over to the end of the small room where some printed flyers were stacked in neat piles on the floor in the far corner.

'I think I'll take about 500,' said Jeanie, as he handed one of the pamphlets to her.

The posters were handwritten. She shared their pride as she read DON'T MESS WITH THE WOMEN in a firm, bold hand, followed by directions for where and at what time to meet for the buses to Johannesburg the next Friday for a national meeting of democratic women's groups over that weekend.

PLEASE DESTROY IMMEDIATELY!!! the pamphlet ended. Strangely, this warning was hardly ever ignored, so the cops very seldom knew what the people were up to. Except when the information landed in the wrong hands. Jeanie knew from her awful time the other night, that the cops had an inkling that something was brewing. She also knew that they did not know exactly what was happening, that they were guessing. And the people would keep them guessing.

'This looks great,' she said, and they did, despite the black lines on the edges where the tired machine had spewed out blobs of ink in protest at being forced to grind away throughout the night. Some of the ink came off on her fingers.

She took a plastic bag full of pamphlets.

'Take extra care my sister,' Joe said with premonition through the slit of the door before he locked it behind her.

By the time she reached the Anglia she had already handed out about 50 of the pamphlets, The rest of the flyers she spread under the carpet in the back before she climbed in behind the steering wheel of the government car, feeling good that their own transport was being used to speed their downfall.

The morning went quickly, enjoyably. Double joy. She enjoyed being the bearer of the good news of the women's meeting, handing out the pamphlets while she did her job. And the joy of her job, nursing post-natal mothers, lingering, talking baby talk to intently staring infants, even getting a few open-mouthed smiles from one or two new-born babies, under the scrutiny of adoring elders.

Retying and cleaning stumps of umbilical cord; checking little bodies and eyes for jaundice; tenderly disinfecting burning outer vaginal areas; enjoying the smells of disinfectant, baby oil and powder, Nurse Dean lived herself into her job. She knew what she was doing, and she did it well. With therapeutic concentration she gave her patients and their babies all the love and care which she had been carefully storing up for the day when she might nurse her own.

When she left the last house, her body sagged into the well-worn driver's seat, pushing down into the comfortable contours of the bucket seat and, like a cat, wriggling complacently, she drove along slowly, looking for a public telephone.

She had decided to spend the rest of the day with her friend, Zogi. There was so much she had to tell her friend. Her face went sad at the thought of what she was to say to Zogi.

She hummed along to the smooth soft jazz coming through the car stereo.

'Manenberg,' she sang the name of the township in whose honour Dollar Brand had written the song, for she was just passing Manenberg, a huge housing estate of council flats.

Then chaos.

'Bloody hell!' someone shouted above blaring car horns. Her heart jumped into her throat.

Her feet were jammed down on the accelerator and brake pedals on the end of unbending legs, nervous back muscles trembling with shock. In wonder she saw the palm of her left hand glued to the gear lever under white knuckles.

The sun had by now turned into a mockingly alive, red bull as it bent down to peer heatedly into her tired eyes through the windscreen. She blinked to shut it out.
Then it dawned on her.

She had actually fallen asleep between one traffic light and the next! Within a distance of less than 100 metres. And this at noon on a weekday.

How she had managed to stop the car an inch from the blue Cortina in front was a mystery. Her reflexes must have taken over, because she could not remember.

She became aware that someone was standing next to her. A pair of blue eyes stared at her through the closed window, from beneath unkempt blond eyebrows. The bronze face was suspended from a thick, beefy neck and out of the deep chest a curse rose up, 'You silly-'

It was the last straw. The body of noble, brave, proud Nurse Dean let go.

At the same time her car engine, which had been holding its breath in idle suspense, gave a cheeky jerk and switched off. The nurse closed her eyes as if to shut out all knowledge of the havoc she had caused. Her tired face puckered up and tears started pouring, uncontrolled, down her cheeks.

What went through the mind of the big white South African ('boers' as they were known – most often with contempt) will never be known.

All that the poor nurse realised, when she again opened her eyes, was that he was walking away without finishing his sentence, leaving her to start up her car, turn left at the traffic lights, stop immediately around the corner and give vent to her feelings, tears now no longer wanting to be held back, trying to wash away the hell and memories of the last two nights.

She felt, before she saw, the big hand on her right shoulder and then heard, 'I'll get you a cup of coffee. Wait here.' He spoke in his language. The deep sounds of the Afrikaans language coming from an Afrikaner sounded richer coming from his deep chest.

He must have followed her. She realised this as she watched him cross the busy street, making his way through heavy traffic to the tearoom on the other side.

All that I need now is for another one of them to be nice to me before gruelling me again, she thought with mistrust, unsure whether to drive away immediately or to obey what sounded like yet another command from a white baas (boss).

At that moment, though, she could not get away if she tried, for her muscles refused to obey.

So, she closed her eyes and suspended time.

# Chapter 5

She was mindlessly staring out of the window when she noticed him coming back across the road carrying two polystyrene cups. His heavy brown boots under faded blue jeans covered muscled calves and thighs. Perhaps a farmer or, God forbid! an undercover cop? The unmatched avocado green cotton shirt neatly tucked in over a surprisingly flat belly revealed a bit of chest covered with more of those thick, blond and curly hairs which covered his head.

She was unable to quell the rapidly rising, bitter tasting, racial bile which welled up in her throat, the result of decades of inherited dislike for the Afrikaner. She found it impossible, in that moment of impotence, to shake off the instant fear she felt by just the look of him.

But she was also deeply upset by the feeling of excitement that trembled down her nervous back. She shivered. What a bundle of contradiction she was. For Nurse Dean also had a secret weakness for hairy men.

His bright smile as he approached her car did not help to settle her nervousness.

'Here you are, nursie. You look tired,' when she rolled down her window. 'Must have worked hard last night, eh?' he said as he gave her one of the warm cups.

Not waiting for her slow brain to produce some sort of polite reply, he strolled back to his jeep which she now saw in her rear-view mirror was parked behind her white Anglia. He drove away with a small toot and a wave of his big hand, leaving thoroughly intimidated Nurse Dean sipping her coffee, trying to readjust her world.

She started up her car and drove away very carefully, putting distance between the strange experience, its uncomfortable ending and the unpredictability of her reactions, as huge and unfamiliar to her as the man she had seen.

She was not, for a long time yet, to know that the strange encounter, somehow and very slowly, had started a new turn in her heart and in her life.

She drove along painstakingly slowly, so slow as to cause an even bigger danger to other road users. She had to find a public telephone from which to phone her relief nurse.

The big, orange telephone booth she was about to pass had about 20 people pushing to get inside. No use getting involved in that queue. She decided rather to pull rank.

She stopped the car in the nearest open space, jumped out and swung her cape over her shoulders, grabbed her bag and ran into the nearest shop.

Inside the shop a pretty, young, blond girl saw her and waited, while a man stood in the corner of the furniture store jingling money in his pockets - or whatever men do with their hands when they are moving them around deep in their trouser pockets Jeanie thought, glancing at him and then smilingly turning to the young woman.

'My bleeper has just gone off and the queue outside the public phone is a mile long. May I use your phone, please?' The girl looked over to the man who must have been the manager of the shop. The man nodded. The girl led Jeanie through into the little office behind the counter.

'Hi, Douglas?' Jeanie asked in answer to the deep voice which answered. 'I've had no new deliveries. I'll bring my report to you later today, ok?' 'Oh, hi Dean!' came the reply. 'Will you give me another hour? I'm just doing one or two little things.'

Oh drat, thought Jeanie, going quiet for a moment, reluctant to stay on call any longer. 'I'm really tired, Douglas,' she said. She could not risk another hour, could not risk having to answer another call for an emergency delivery. 'I almost rammed into a car this morning, falling asleep while driving,' hoping this would convince the woman that she could not go on working.

But Nurse Douglas seemed not to have heard the last bit. Or if she did, she ignored Jeanie, for she shouted into the background 'Turn the music down,' and then, into the receiver, 'what was that again, Jeanie?'

'It's alright,' Jeanie said despondently, suspecting that Douglas was just a little drunk and needed to shake it off, as she had been rather heavily into the bottle lately. 'I'll stay on for a while longer. What do you want me to do?'

'There's a new mum in Lansdowne who was discharged this morning. Mind checking on her before you knock off, Dean?' asked Douglas.

'Ok then,' said Jeanie, reaching for some paper on the untidy counter in front of her. Douglas gave her the name and address of the patient and she wrote it down.

It will take my mind off myself for a bit longer, she thought, as she replaced the receiver and walked back through the shop, offering to pay the nice young lady, who with a shake of the head refused payment and with a smile saw Jeanie out into the sunshine.

Glancing at her watch, Jeanie saw it was just after one in the afternoon. She drove through Guguletu on the open Klipfontein Road to Lansdowne. Time for a quick cat nap, she thought, and she stopped the car off the busy road where she would be safe under some trees, locked the doors, leaned forward over the steering wheel, and fell into a deep sleep for fifteen minutes.

Refreshed, she woke up. To be hit by a nasty realisation.

In the paralyzing fear of a moment at about 4 o'clock on Tuesday night (no – Wednesday morning) – when the interrogation had become almost unbearable, she had promised them that she would telephone them to say where Zogi was. She had at the time got away with pretending to them that she did not know, but could ask friends where Zogi was.

She would have to speak with Zogi, then phone them, or they might come and pick her up again.

Fear crept slowly up her spine as she started her car up. She felt its tentacles in every little nerve end. Her toes pulled up tightly inside her shoes.

She had better get hold of Zogi immediately. But she could not call Zogi from a private telephone. Not only because people might overhear, but because Zogi's telephone was definitely bugged, and calls could be traced. This time it meant standing in the lengthy queue in the infernal sun for twenty minutes before it was her turn.

'I'm waiting,' was all she said when she heard her friend's voice on the other end of the line. This had been done many times before and Zogi knew that she was to get herself to a public telephone and dial through to the public telephone at which Jeanie would be waiting. Zogi knew the number. This way they knew that if their conversation leaked, they had done their best.

She went to their pre-arranged telephone booth, and waited about ten minutes before the call came through. Luckily there were no people waiting there. Most of them had trekked to work at six that morning and only a handful of housewives and some *ou rookers* (literally translated, 'old smokers') – unemployed men who hang around in the streets in Cape Town – a few of them were seen around.

'Jeanie, you ok?' her friend asked with deep concern. She must have heard, via the efficient bush telegraph, what had happened to Jeanie.

'Yea. I must see you very urgently.' Knowing that whatever else Zogi had to do that morning, she would postpone, even going to a funeral, for comrades do not use the word urgent carelessly.

'Ok. Meet you in about 15 minutes.' It was not necessary to mention the place, as they knew exactly where to meet.

As Jeanie walked along to the Catholic church on the corner of 15th Avenue and Halt Road, she once again marvelled at the security which comes from little things. Little things like her friend's total trust in her and Father Goodman's sanctuary of a backroom, always available for people to hide out or meet in, no matter what time of day or night.

It was better not to take the car where she was going now, so she left it parked on the forecourt of a service station, where it would be safe until she returned.

When she arrived there, Zogi was waiting. How lucky I am to have you as a friend, she thought as she hugged her thin, small, beautiful, 20-year-old friend. Untangling herself from Zogi's long hair, Jeanie Dean's day suddenly felt much warmer and brighter.

Together they went into the little room with its stacked chairs and blankets and settled down on a cushion each on the floor. An unplanned moment of silence followed, while they sat there just loving each other for a short while. No pretentions, no need to act grown-up or wise, only a mutual respect here.

A bond of complete friendship.

'They followed me home on Tuesday night on my way from a call,' Jeanie started. Zogi knew who they were. Explanations were not needed. And, of course, she was not shocked or repulsed that someone close to her was involved with the police.

'Six of them in three cars. Crowded me off the street in Epping Avenue and told me to follow them to the Epping Police Station.'

Zogi had not yet said a word. Jeanie looked at her friend and admired her for her calmness.

Much shorter than Jeanie, Zogi was also very slightly built. Her baggy blue trousers and big black t-shirt made her look even smaller. Her close-set hazel eyes were looking at her older sister, as she fondly called Jeanie, with concern, beside a slightly freckled, straight, finely shaped nose. Jeanie wondered why bloody Pretoria had chosen to class Zogi's family as Indian when she probably looked more Irish than most people from up there. And with brains, too. Zogi held a master's degree in music and was a pianist of concert hall quality, but, of course, would never get to perform in the philharmonic orchestra, because she was not white.

God forgive our country, Jeanie thought. Almost as if she could read Jeanie's thoughts, Zogi's naturally pink, slightly pouted lips went up in a slight smile.

'Did you recognise any of them?'

'Not really. I think I saw Van der Merwe. Not sure though.' Van der Merwe was one of the local security police's most vicious cads.

'Any idea why they picked you up?'

'I think they wanted to know what was happening over the weekend with the group going up to Jo'burg' (Johannesburg), 'who organised it and so on,'

Jeanie said. Watching Zogi's reaction carefully, she continued, 'I'm sorry, Zogi, I admitted to them that the two of us were involved in the planning. They knew that we were together at the meeting last Friday, showed me photos.'

What a blessed feeling, though, that her friend just nodded in complete understanding without a half-expected but surely you could have said... Jeanie really appreciated the sensitivity of this friend of hers. Quite irresistibly she quickly slotted Zogi under one of her secret, favourite labels, 'She who knows but knows not that she knows,' for Zogi's common sense, of which she was quite unaware, exceeded that of most of their acquaintances. Jeanie respected her young friend very much.

'Did you have to sign anything?' asked Zogi.

'No.' Thank God it had not yet come to signing trumped-up confessions! Meetings of more than 2 people were banned at the time, unless leave to hold the meeting was obtained in advance from a magistrate. Of course, their meeting had had no exemption.

What reason would one give to a magistrate for a meeting to plan a protest?

'O damn, Zogi, I feel so soiled and contaminated!' Jeanie started sobbing as it all flooded back.

'Feel like talking about it?' asked Zogi quietly, without the presumption that she had a right to know.

Both of them knew that not all could possibly be said. She did trust this friend of hers completely, but also sadly realised the stupidity of endangering her friend's life. Not only Zogi's, but all of them. It was better not to know some things, for then it cannot be forced out of you under interrogation.

Jeanie sat quietly for a minute, staring at the dark blue tiles on the floor. In her abstraction she suddenly realised that she was counting the tiles and had reached twenty-five before her mind, again, became flooded with the sickness of the experience. She needed to let go, to talk.

A shudder went through her body. 'They used a black cop first –' she started quietly. 'I didn't know him. He was with me for about an hour from five in the morning. At first they made me just sit there for about two hours on the floor. Then he came in,' she continued softly.

## Chapter 6

She saw again the smirk on his face as he slammed, and locked, the door behind him. Towering over her, he had bent down in mock gallantry, offering her his hand so that she could stand up.

Ignoring his hand, she got up and moved a step back to avoid the stink of old beer which rushed out over the big blob of chewing gum stuck on brown teeth, out through large black lips, and into her face.

She would have liked to smack the disgusting grin off his face. She stood there, waiting for the next move.

Putting his arm around her waist, in friendship he said, 'Sit down, my beauty. Let's talk about this silly business.'

She pulled herself away from him and sat down on the other side of the table on the only chair – which he had brought in with him. He remained standing in physical, but not mental, dominance.

'Come, come now. You know why you were brought here. Why not make it short and sweet then you can go home sooner?'

'I've got no idea why I'm here,' she said, sullenly, staring at him with absolutely no response to his pathetic innuendo, or fatherliness, or whatever he thought he was throwing out to her.

'Listen, my pretty. The people here know that something is cooking up in Jo'burg. They also know who is at the bottom of it. And you know how silly it is to be brave and act as a shield for these communists. Now, all I want you to do is to tell me what was happening last weekend and we will let you go.'

'I don't know what you're talking about,' Jeanie said stubbornly. 'Oh, don't you?' He went quiet, trying to stare her down. 'Then what were you doing with that Anthony woman from Paarl the other day?'

Oh hell. How did they know that she had met Doreen? She was one person whom it was best not to be seen around with. Doreen was under a banning order in Paarl because of her immense influence amongst the workers. She was a trade unionist. She was not allowed by law to leave the municipal boundaries of Paarl. But she had secretly travelled to Cape Town and Jeanie had met her. She was a respected activist in the women's movement and had wide experience.

They needed Doreen to give a talk, but it was too dangerous for her to travel to Johannesburg and break her banning order. So, Jeanie had recorded her message, which they were going to play over loudspeakers at the meeting in Johannesburg. News of her talk was already out and would attract thousands of women who admired her, to the meeting.

But no way was Jeanie going to admit that she had met Doreen Anthony. If she admitted having seen Doreen in Cape Town, Doreen might be in for a very long stretch in jail for breaking her banning order.

So, then she knew why they were so anxious to find out what next weekend was about. If they suspected that Doreen, with her national influence, was involved, then they would definitely be panicking.

To stall for time, Jeanie said, 'Who? What Anthony woman?'

Then his tone changed. 'Don't waste my time, nurse. You bloody well know who I'm talking about. And we know that you saw her last week. I've got written statements from others who saw you.'

Show me your statements first, she thought. He's lying. 'They're lying,' she said, rather convincingly, as she was later to tell her friends.

Over the next hour came the flattery. About being intelligent, admired and educated. The bribes, about the great job lined up for her husband and promotional prospects for her, and much more. Promises as old as Table Mountain itself.

Then the threats, of indefinite imprisonment, no food. Threats of assault, with graphic descriptions of how these would be carried out.

And when none of these evoked any response, anger and pure dastardliness. Insults and swearing poured from the man's mouth in a continuous barrage for about an hour while she just sat there, like a statue, helpless with fear, staring at nothing.

Jeanie's fear of physical violence was her weakness, but also her strength. For outside of direct attack, she could handle intimidation. Insults and threats no longer penetrated. She had received her fair share and more from her husband over many years, and she blocked out the man's blaspheming with not much effort. She had become almost immune.

Physical violence, though, was quite another thing. To her the ultimate form of humiliation was to be physically assaulted.

Eventually the savage, as she had by now came to regard him, ran out of expletives. Even vileness has its limitations. Eventually he angrily spat out his chewing gum, missing her face by centimetres, and stormed out of the room.

But at least he had not touched her.

The sudden silence was short lived, for suddenly, loud music blared out above her head, discordant violins, trumpets, screeching metal, a deafening clash of drums. The sound was so sudden and magnified, reverberating from wall to wall in the small room, that she jumped up in fright.

Where the noise was coming from, she did not know. In fact, she did not even look up to see where the speakers were, but sat down on the floor to get her pounding heart to relax. She closed her eyes, covering her ears with her hands in the classical, in this case, pose of see no evil, hear no evil.

I actually must have managed to go into meditation, for I forget how it ended, she now realised with wonderment.

Her young friend sat quietly listening, not moving, not asking any questions, making no comments.

Jeanie could not tell it all. The details of her meeting with Doreen Anthony need not be told, for Zogi had not been at that meeting and it was better for her not to know what they had discussed.

And neither was she able to speak to her friend about the ultimate humiliation, that part of the horrible experience which was so intimate and shameful that she could never reveal it to anyone, not even to a girlfriend as close to her as Zogi was.

Jeanie suddenly could go no further. The pain became too much for her. The hurt churned in her empty stomach. No further words could come. Choking down this suddenly uncontrollable feeling of total frustration and anger and completely overwhelmed by the treachery of it all, she bent forward. With head almost touching her crossed legs, she allowed her tears to flow.

This time she was in a safe place, with a person whom she trusted. She let go. But the grief magnified the bitter memories.

Two white cops came in after that with more threats, lies and a typed statement, trying to force her to sign something she had not even read. Back-handed slaps when she'd closed her eyes so as not to return the hatred she was receiving from them. Knuckles poking into her ribs which still felt sore and tender. These things she was unable to speak about.

Neither could she even think of repeating the swearing, and the deep feelings of degradation, which were way beyond words.

## Chapter 7

Confused, Jeanie woke up. A loud bang had catapulted her out of a rambling nightmare.

She sat up, trying to focus, for it felt like she was still sitting waiting in the car under a disappearing moon, car lights off, engine dead. A light breeze of relief coming through the open window, slipping through the silence of dawn, sweeping anxiety away from her sweating face, as she had continued to sit and wait at dawn one morning.

She remembered sitting there watching the morning sun slowly rise through the trees on either side of the road, waiting for Bruce to arrive. Bruce, her first love, who had been killed on the banks of the Orange River. Bruce, 18 years old when she was 16, to whom she had vowed her eternal virgin love. Bruce, who had died after falling and being crushed under his own diamond digger on the banks of the Orange River.

Yet the man who walked from between the trees looked and walked like Bruce. He kissed her through the open car window before he opened the back door and put the case of money and pamphlets on the back seat.

She started the car up immediately and turned onto the freeway, heading for the quickest route down from the Botswana border, through Southwest Africa, through the Northern Cape, down south.

The two of them sang and rejoiced all the way, singing together in the car while the engine purred, celebrating their success.

'Remember how they went to your flat in Hillbrow to search – and found nothing?' she asked him and they burst out into fresh laughter.

His niece had phoned him to go with Jeanie to Botswana to collect the money from a safe house occupied by the underground movement. The security police must have received garbled intelligence from its spies about the arrangement, and had gone to his flat to do a search. They, of course, found nothing, but their presence had been the alarm for urgent action.

'That was some brilliant planning done there, Comrade!' he winked into the windscreen which into which flying mosquitoes collided, to die onto the glass magnet of death. Jeanie could hardly see through the windscreen and had to stop to clean it every thirty minutes.

Nothing mattered, nothing could interrupt their joy. They had made it!

When the call had come through that the money had been delivered safely in Botswana, Jeanie had not hesitated to offer to go, for her car was new and had not yet been linked to her legal name, for she had registered it under a false surname – for exactly that reason.

The 5,000 km border between South Africa and its northern neighbours is easy to cross, because it has only a few isolated border posts. The fields, bridges and rivers between South Africa and its neighbours make it almost impossible to stop families walking safely across in their thousands every year, fleeing war and persecution and in search of safety and work.

It had been easy for the two of them to part ways just before the Ngoma bridge in Southwest Africa. Her car was, of course, carefully searched – even the carpet in the back was force-lifted - and the back seat was upended in their long search before she was waived through.

She'd used her sister's passport that night. For, although her car was not yet under the radar of the security police, her passport certainly was.

'Borrowing' passports was done regularly in those dark days when you could be found guilty of crimes which carried the death penalty simply by association. If you were seen with someone who had committed an offence, then you were already guilty before you were charged, and the onus was on you to prove your non-guilt – not on the prosecution to find you guilty.

A second, clean, passport was a necessity for those who were cross border runners in the fight for freedom.

He had walked miles away from the border post and crossed over beyond the fence to meet up with her in Botswana on the other side.

When they drove back with the contraband in the boot, he once again left her just outside the border post at *Skilpadshek* (Afrikaans for tortoise gate).

He, her comrade, who had protected her and saved her so many times over the years. He had served his time as a bank robber and was recruited into the underground movement in jail, he'd told her that first time they met in a shebeen in Johannesburg six, seven years ago.

He, her bank robber friend and comrade, could smell a cop and was known as *Stinker* because of his history. He acted as an informal bodyguard to many of them when they needed protection.

How many, many times had Stinker not stood outside a midnight meeting as the lookout and how many times had he not correctly identified someone's 'friend' who had come along to be recruited, only to turn out to be the spy for the security police whom Stinker had accused them of being?

Jeanie remembered telling him about that day when an undercover policeman – a colleague - had approached her in hospital to spy on one of their colleagues, a young medical intern. She had agreed, so that she could do her own checks. It was Stinker who had immediately recognised the snitch. 'Definitely a cop – just look at his shoes and the way he stands.' And he'd been right!

Recruiting him, the liberation movement had received in return more than its trust when it had trusted criminal, white man Stinker. How all of them admired him!

That night, walking the 10 kilometres to cross back over the fields into Southwest Africa (now called Namibia), Stinker, the ex-bank robber, had again proved his worth. Jeanie had given him the suitcase packed full of US dollars plus a backpack full of banned materials to smuggle back into the country.

Their bank-robber colleague had not taken a cent from the suitcase and had met her on the South African side of the border with all that money. How she still admires him!

Her dream did not separate the then from the now, so Jeanie sat up in her lonely cell, wiping sweat from her brow with her skirt with a heart beating above the noise in her longing to see Stinker again.

## Chapter 8

And then, worse, much worse than the mental assaults, that night in the cell, the ultimate degradation, so intimate and shameful that she could never even hint of it to anyone alive, which she vowed to take to the grave with her.

Jeanie's period started during that morning, and she had nothing to protect herself with.

Slightly at first, she felt the wetness. She had no idea what to do, could not call out to anyone. The door to the small room was locked. She would have to wait until the next idiot turned up. But how was she to explain – what could she say? Her world was then truly hanging upside down, suspended by shame and embarrassment.

Her next inquisitor was a squat, ugly male with a bald head and nasty moustache, which covered a cruel upper lip. Full of unpleasantness and self-importance, he came into the room, hiking up trousers which were already stretching over a round belly.

By this time Jeanie was sitting on the floor with a heel under her, trying to stop the flow of blood.

He did not bother to sit down, but just stood, towering over her, his almost square head and round body blocking out the light from the little window behind him. He stood looking down at her, intimidating her, just stood there staring at her for a long time.

At last Jeanie could hold back no longer. 'I need a toilet,' she almost whispered, looking up at him. She remembered now how the bastard smiled, simply smiled at her, an evil smile, while he just stood there, forcing her to cast her eyes down. Before her eyes left his face, she saw him rotating his head slowly to the bucket standing in the corner of the room, his depraved grin glued to his face with malevolence.

Jeanie sank into stubbornness, her only defence, repeating, as she had learnt to do so many times while being assaulted at home, repeating deep inside her, trying to still her shattered insides, you can touch me but you cannot break my spirit! She kept her head down, all nerves on edge, keeping her mind fixed on her little mantra, waiting for him to reach down and haul her to her feet.

After a long silence she heard him walk to the door, open it, walk out and lock it. He had not said a word to her.

As soon as she heard him walk away, Jeanie fumbled with her uniform, opened the top buttons, still sitting on that floor, wriggled herself out of her bra, stood up quickly, and stuffed her bra into her knickers to stop the flow of blood. The bra saved her until, hours later, she stuffed it into the waste disposal bin, wrapped in toilet paper in a public toilet, before she drove home.

She'd stopped off at a shop to buy sanitary towels, one of which she swapped for the bra in the toilet after they eventually released her.

# Chapter 9

The disembowelled memories bombarded her mind when she sank into unconscious exhaustion.

Compounded by Gregory's viciousness the next night, her memories were almost too much to bear. Her lungs emptied themselves through sobs so deep, they threatened to tear her chest apart. Her slender body sensibly, unconsciously, rocked itself back and forth on the floor of Father Goodman's small sanctuary in the back of the Catholic church. With the knowledge of ages, as mothers do without learning, her body rocked itself, accessing ancient streams of comfort, gently easing her pain.

And then she smelt Zogi, felt her warm body consoling her back, as her friend knelt behind her, with arms folded about her and head buried into Jeanie's back, in wordless understanding.

'They…they were at it all day…until… till… Zogi. I…I – I'm so sorry! – I told them that the two of us, you and me, were organising the whole thing,' feeling that she had let her dear friend down.

Zogi turned Jeanie to face her and, with a smile of wisdom, said, 'Well, the good thing is that it is not true, so let them think us more important that we are. That way they will stop looking for anyone else.'

Wisdom broke the spell of sadness and they both started laughing, softly at first, then with relief, joyfully celebrating the small victory.

'I'm supposed to phone them to tell them where you are…' Jeanie said, suddenly remembering.

'Blast them. Let's not waste any more time talking about idiots. How 'bout the two of us go an' get lost in the crowds tonight?' said the wise young one.

'Yea. Blast the cops.' Jeanie said, 'We won't phone them. They won't find us in the crowds anyway.'

They arranged to meet at a café in the city later on.

A revived Jeanie arrived at her new patient's house about fifteen minutes later. Seeing Zogi had done wonders for her, although not much had changed. She felt light and was looking forward to their evening together. Gregory would be away for two more days, and that was enough to give anyone a lift of spirits.

Ronalda Khan lived in one of the more affluent suburbs of Lansdowne, a 'coloured' suburb. The spacious cleanliness of the Khan home was very different from the little council flats where most of the other mothers lived.

She spent a pleasant twenty minutes cuddling the baby, giving Ronalda tips on how to bathe, breastfeed and change her first baby.

On her way home, Jeanie stopped in Lansdowne Road at a shop to buy a cool drink, when a plump woman, in her late forties, approached her. 'Hello, Nurse Dean,' the ugly, loose floral pinafore and flat, tattered sandals she was wearing making her look much older.

'Oh, hi Mrs. Delaney. How are you?' Jeanie was very pleased to see her. She had helped Mrs Delaney through three of her seven pregnancies and births.

'I'm really glad to see you, nurse.' Mrs. Delaney shook her head, her unruly hair, now almost completely grey, encircling her smiling face like a halo in front of the sun. She rested a well-worn hand, pink and raw, on her abdomen, giving Jeanie a message which the nurse immediately understood.

'When?' Jeanie asked, not sure of whether to show pleasure or surprise.

Mrs. Delaney frowned slightly, but gave Jeanie a wan smile as she said, 'This was really a surprise for both myself and the old man, nurse. It's coming in three months' time.'

'That should be about the end of March, early April,' Jeanie interrupted.

The lady nodded, continuing as if the actual event were unimportant. 'The poor chap. He's working so hard. And now this,' as if she were the cause of it all.

Jeanie was at a total loss for words and stood looking at the woman, feeling sorry that life could be so very unfair. These people could not afford any more children, did not want anymore. Yet…

Mrs. Delaney's giggle cut through her thoughts.

'Know what I did when I found out?' she said, leaning forward, her soft, warm belly pushing up against Jeanie's lower arm. 'I got completely motherless on a bottle of gin while the old man was at work. I almost fainted in one hot bath after another.' Her smile changed into a mirthless laugh, attractive laughter lines about her eyes. But the detached laugh did not remove the worry from her eyes.

Jeanie did not laugh. She felt rather sorry for Mrs. Delaney. 'Well, I suppose there is nothing you can do about it,' she said sensibly. 'Miscarriages don't happen that easily.'

Mrs Delaney nodded. 'In a way I'm glad it didn't happen. I would never have been able to live with myself if it did. You know how strict the church is,' with a sign of the cross. 'God will provide. Anyway, nature must do its job,' she said with meaning, with an earnest frown. As nature had done.

'You will, of course, help me again, won't you, nurse?' she asked.

'Sure, of course. Just give them my name at the clinic. I look forward to being there. You are one of my best patients. You make it so easy. In fact, I don't think you even need me!' she said to comfort Mrs. Delaney as they said goodbye and Jeanie walked into the shop.

She drove straight back to her home and parked the Anglia on her side of the garage. Gregory's Volvo reminded her of her temporary freedom, and she whistled happily as she went into the house. She quickly changed into jeans and a light sweater, leaving her thick African hair uncombed. Once a day is enough of that agony.

Going into the kitchen, she cut off a big piece of cheese and munched on it while she telephoned Nurse Douglas to report. Then, feeling like a schoolgirl just released from boarding school at the end of term, she set off to meet Zogi in town.

Jeanie arrived when the sun was almost setting, and hundreds of people were moving around the grand parade opposite the city hall on that bright summer's day. She was slightly late and rushed to the spot just outside the back door to the big post office building, where she had arranged to meet Zogi, expecting to find her waiting.

Zogi was not there. After waiting for thirty minutes, Jeanie gave up.

She did not know that the next time she and Zogi met, it would be under circumstances far worse than what she had been through over the last few days.

She decided to take a slow walk down the upper main road towards Woodstock, as the evening was fresh and she felt safe amongst the crowds, when she heard singing. The music was coming through massive speakers outside a big tent. There were quite a lot of people standing outside the entrance and Jeanie joined them, unsure as to whether to go further in under the massive tarpaulin, which must have held about a thousand people.

The singing flowed from one song into another without interruption. A band was set up on the raised stage and

Jeanie soon became engrossed in the excellent, jazzy beat, admiring the musicians who entered into the music with energy and sweat as if they were being paid for it.

People were pushing in from outside, and soon she was forced forward along the right aisle. People were standing, hands raised, swinging to the rhythm of the beat.

Jeanie became quite carried away with the mood of the place and she forgot about Zogi. She had come in on the meeting almost at the end, for a man walked up onto the stage and raised his hands, indicating to the crowd to sit down. The place went quiet.

The man stood still for a moment, looking around, then he walked forward and spoke into the microphone at the centre of the stage.

'Brothers and sisters,' he said, 'We can feel God's spirit move in our presence here tonight. If there is anyone in the room tonight who would like to be healed, we ask you to come forward for prayer.'

'Praise the Lord!' the crowd exalted as the music started up, a deep, soulful moan starting slowly and building up as the choir took up the mood with 'Don't let this moment pass you by. Jesus is waiting with his arms open wide.' Swinging, clapping, with hands raised, eyes closed, the crowd joined the choir, some waving their arms, bodies swaying in exaltation.

The music penetrated her, and Jeanie's need propelled her forward magnetically, in hope and expectation for a miracle, as she knelt down and felt hands on her head in prayer.

A head, always on the lookout for opportunities, which had seen a chance for yet another cure for her childlessness.

## Chapter 10

The thought entered Jeanie's head quite unexpectedly one evening. She was going to ask Gregory, come what may, she decided, already starting to tremble at the thought of saying anything to him which might upset the fragile politeness which had settled in between them over the past few weeks.

One gynaecological test had followed another. Painful and embarrassing, as she exposed the most intimate details of her female physiology and sexual failures to clinical, wise old men, too busy taking notes to hear the deep cry of pain beneath her words.

Late one evening, after yet another gynaecological examination, Jeanie approached Gregory. He was sitting in his chair lost in television.

'I've been back to Dr Freedman again today,' she said.

'Really,' he replied absentmindedly, not turning his head. Not making it easy for her.

She was determined not to be stopped. 'He said again that he could find nothing physically wrong with me.' Holding her breath.

Jeanie had spent much that day alone after she had been to see the doctor. The monotonous, drizzling autumn rain had let up for the day, and she had grabbed the quick opportunity to drive up along the scenic De Waal Drive, where she parked her car and took a slow walk up the foot paths.

She had discovered a cave about fifty feet up the mountain and sat there worrying. Gone was her usual enjoyment at the incredible sight of the pink reflections the rising sun made on individual dew drops nestling between the determined, upright little green needles of infant pine trees, the older members of their families standing above them protectively, shielding them from the extremities of the weather.

She'd sat there alone for a good hour, a new thought building up in her head, gazing through the remnants of the thick mist which flowed down the mountain like a tablecloth in the distance.

She had made up her mind well before she walked down to the car that, come what may, today she was going to speak with Gregory, to get rid of the nagging doubt which had come up in her mind.

'Doctor said again that he could find nothing physically wrong with me.' This time there was a reaction. He jerked his head towards her and stared at her for a long moment. Before he spoke, Jeanie knew, by the way he pulled his lips, what his response would be.

'What's that got to do with me?'

'What's it got to do with you?' she echoed, feeling silly.

'Yes, what's it got to do with me!'

'Well – everything, Greg. We are trying to have a baby together, aren't we?' 'Jeanie, I'm tired of you and your doctors, I am sick of the unspoken suggestion that I'm the one to blame for the fact that you cannot fall pregnant.'

'But Greg –' she started, then went silent. She wanted to say but I had a pregnancy before I met you! I miscarried ... that time...But of course she did not say this.

'I'm not suggesting that you are to blame,' she quickly defended herself, and him, for that matter.

'What exactly are you saying, then?' He knew, of course he knew. She had told him that she had been pregnant with her first lover, well before she agreed to get married to him.

'I, well...um, I mean –,' she stuttered.

'Come on, Jeanie. Shall I say it for you? If there is nothing wrong with you, then I need to have myself examined, as surely there must be something wrong with one of us...Is that what you're saying?' now standing up, facing her.

Jeanie dropped her eyes, went silent.

'Jeanie, Jeanie,' his tone had gone softer. 'You know that this is not the right time for us to go into this whole saga again.' She flinched. 'I'm having terrible problems at work and things need to settle down first before we get side tracked.'

'I didn't know you were having problems at work,' she looked at him, relief flooding her face at having something else to talk about. 'What happened?'

'Well, you know that young chap I told you about who came into our department about six months ago? They're promoting him to manager of our department. And after I've been with the company for so many years.

'That's unfair,' she said, for want of something to say, relieved that an explosion had been avoided.

She was getting more and more depressed as the winter set in, moving under a constant tiredness which would not go away. She had not heard from Zogi either and this nagged at the bottom of everything she did.

# Chapter 11

It was Gregory who first gave her an idea about what was happening with Zogi.

The tension between Jeanie and Gregory was constant. She felt that she was always having to walk on eggshells when around him.

Very early one morning, while she was still in bed, Gregory could not find a clean pair of underpants to wear. He pulled out drawers and emptied their contents in confusion on the floor, looking for a way to irritate her. All she heard was the backend of a mutter from under his breath '…laziest woman…'.

Jeanie snapped. She could not hold back. 'Cleaning, cooking, sweeping, ironing. That's all you people know about. Go and talk to your mother. Ask her to do it for you…' she screamed as she jumped out of bed, running down the passage towards the bathroom.

'You leave my mother out of this!' his shout propelled her down the passage.

By then she was not able to stay on the side of reason. She turned around, ran back and stood in the open bedroom doorway. Then, totally unreasonably, forgetting she was the one who had started shouting first, she ended lamely, 'God, I'm tired!'

'You're so damned impossible, you silly bitch. Why don't you fuck off and go and live with your junkie friend?'

Jeanie froze. 'Don't put my friends in your camp!' she said, but she had a feeling he was talking about Zogi.

Gregory looked at her, his eyes narrowed, breathing heavily, lips pulled together tightly in mounting anger.

'You know full well who I'm talking about. That slut is always drugged up to her eyeballs. What's wrong with you? Everyone knows it except you,' he jeered. He saw that he had shocked her into silence.

She turned back to the bathroom and eventually heard him leave the house without saying goodbye.

She was riddled with doubt. Jeanie wanted to be true and loyal to her friend. She desperately wanted to get to the bottom of Gregory's spiteful allegations, but did not really know what to do about it. She could not get hold of Zogi and even if she did see her, how could she straight out ask Zogi if she had a drug problem? What sense would there be in confronting her friend about something which might be totally untrue?

It would kill their friendship, for there is nothing worse than seeing doubt creep into the minds of people whom one trusts, whom one thinks understands you completely – and then to see their doubt. Doubts were trapped in her head, spinning around, moving about like black clouds ahead of a storm.

The last thing she wanted was to lose the comfort and understanding of Zogi's friendship. That would be a loss which Jeanie did not think she would be able to live through right now. Especially as her own life was in such confusion and seemed to be heading for a major collapse.

Perhaps Zogi was avoiding her .... but then friends have a right to their privacy ... but what if Zogi did have a problem and I do not help her? What kind of friend am I to stand by while my friend is in trouble without doing something about it?

After much anguish Jeanie finally made up her mind. She would rather risk losing her friend than to find out, when it might be too late, that Zogi was too deep into drugs and unable to clean up on her own.

She decided, just in case things had changed, to call the house where Zogi lived.

Still hoping against hope that Zogi might herself answer the phone, Jeanie heard the phone ringing, expecting Zogi to laugh her questions away and to say that 'Gregory can't help being a fart, Jeanie,' as she had so often teased Jeanie.

The person who answered the phone at the house where Zogi had been sharing with three others said, matter of factly, 'Zogi's not here. She's gone to Jo'burg.'

'When?'

'Don't know, we have not seen her for a few months.'

'When you expecting her back?'

'No idea. There's another girl moving into her room to help us pay the rent. She probably won't come back here.'

Jeanie felt slightly cheated by Zogi's disappearance. Why had she not called to say she was not coming back? On the other hand, it was quite characteristic of Zogi to just go with whatever was happening. Something interesting must have come up in the line of a job, perhaps.

Or, maybe she'd met a man in Jo'burg and decided to try out living there for a while? Not likely. Zogi's parents lived in Johannesburg and they were very strict Muslims. No chance Zogi would move in with a man where her parents might get to know about it.

Alone at home one rainy Sunday afternoon, Jeanie wanted to make some notes and was looking for a pen, which she could not find anywhere. Gregory's briefcase was standing in the corner of the dining room and she hunted inside it for one.

Her hand came up out of the front pocket with a beautiful golden chain, a brilliant cluster of diamonds burning into her palm, the shape of a Star of David.

I'm sure I've seen this pendant before – she frowned at it. She could not remember where, or when, she had seen it.

So that's why I've not seen him around – working, indeed! The sod must be having an affair! The pendant belonged to a woman, possibly at his work. How could she have been so blind? Of course, the affair must have been carrying on for quite a few months, she now realised.

There had been so many nights when she had been out on all-night calls, when she would telephone home to say she would be delayed. Most times he had not been at home.

Her feelings were mixed. The events of the last few months had left her almost immune to what Gregory did with his life. In fact, she found it rather crazy, but she was rather amused right then. Later, she knew, she would use this bit of information to maximum effect. Right now, she was rather pleased that she had another good, strong weapon to use.

So, she hid the pendant and said nothing.

Jeanie enjoyed watching Gregory hunt frantically for it about three nights later. Still, she said nothing. She was having fun, seeing him going through every spot he could think of in the house to find the thing. He would stand quite still at times, frowning, not answering her innocent 'Can I help you, Greg?', stalling for time.

It happened a few weeks later, when Jeanie's car had broken down and she took a bus to the city. She was in Adderley Street late in the afternoon and decided, on an impulse, to take a walk to Gregory's car and meet him for a lift home.

She knew where he parked his car and took a slow walk-through Government Avenue and the Gardens, enjoying the beautiful surroundings. Past the Houses of Parliament, the Cape Town museum, she enjoyed walking through what she called her little city.

As she came up to the Volvo, Jeanie could not believe her eyes. She was coming up from behind the car and saw the lovely, slim head from behind. Beautiful, straight, light brown hair was hanging over the back of the front passenger seat.

Heart pounding and suddenly quite angry, Jeanie walked up to the car and knocked on the passenger window.

Their eyes met in common surprise. Beautiful green eyes looked into hers in shock. In her anger Jeanie had to admit that Gregory really knew how to pick the finest objects. The pity is that she is much younger than I am, Jeanie thought, her feelings immediately switching, feeling old and unattractive.

It took a moment for the girl to roll down the window.

Neither of them had said anything so far and it gave Jeanie a chance to get her act together. While she mulled over how best to handle the situation to make a maximum impact, she saw all of the well attired lady's legs, a little black leather skirt which was riding up slim thighs. Precisely modelled breasts cheekily threatened to burst through the feminine black silk, open necked blouse she was wearing. Jeanie hated black silk forever after that.

Two twenty-three carat gold chains were dangling in the cleavage into which Jeanie stared with female jealousy. A matching, heavy gold bracelet slid down her fine wrist as she coquettishly put her hands, red fingernails, perfectly manicured, down on her lap to pull her mini skirt a bit further down. Respect for old age – Jeanie thought, not sparing herself.

Jeanie with her unkempt, uncombed hair, which she had forgotten about since that morning, long skirt and boots, reject army coat, stood dumbfounded for a moment. Unconsciously she pushed the ends of her right hand under the big lapel of her coat to hide her short, no-nonsense nails from the girl's critical gaze.

'Hi. Remember me? Jeanie Dean.' All very civilized.

'Hello. I'm Miranda.'

'Yes, I know.' Jeanie's voice went higher, stretched like a bow before hitting its target. 'Waiting for Gregory?'

'Yeah.'

'Been waiting long?'

'No, I've just arrived.'

Jeanie's throat closed up. She wanted to scream. How the hell did you get into the car, got his keys have you! Perhaps even a key to our front door.

Sense took over. Jeanie, quietly but firmly, said to her husband's lover, 'You must know who I am, don't you?' A nod.

And on the spur of the moment, 'Did Gregory tell you that we were in the process of a divorce?' 'Yes.' The lying sod!

'When did he say it was going to go through?'

'He said the next court hearing is sometime next month.'

So that's how the wind blows. Well, might as well make her dreams turn into reality.

'Then why do you not wait for the divorce to be finalised before carrying on with him?' spite creeping into her voice.

No reply.

'Listen, Miranda. Whether the divorce goes through or not is immaterial to the problems you are heading for. Now that I know about you, you are not going to get out of this that easily.'

She paused, staring intently at the girl, struggling to make up something which would sound threatening enough. 'I'm going to get my lawyer to write you a letter and I'm claiming every penny you have off you. Understand?' Just a shot out of the blue.

Obviously scared, the girl turned her head the other way. She said nothing. The blood slowly crept up her cheeks in embarrassment.

## Chapter 12

Jeanie stared at Miranda for a moment, a strange feeling coming over her. Although she was angry with Gregory for having an affair, the feeling she had for the girl was almost one of sympathy.

'You work with Gregory?'

'No, I don't,' Miranda said, turning her head slowly to look up into Jeanie's face.

'What kind of work do you do?'

No reply. 'That means that you're not earning a living, yes?' Silence.

'Gregory keeping you?' Spite is hard to hide. 'Well, if you want to be sullen about your own sins, that's your affair. Just let me know when you want him to move in with you, then I'll pack his bags. Or did you think you'd be moving into my house after the divorce?' This slipped out unintentionally.

Jeanie turned her back and left the disquieted girl to meet her lover, feeling quite good about the meeting. The girl was obviously quite silly and had not even bothered to find out much about her lover. Beautiful she might be, thought Jeanie spitefully, but she had to come a long way to match up to my type of girl. She does not know what she's up against. But then, I will probably not even fight her. I am so sick of Gregory and his pitiful life.

Whether or not the girl ever told Gregory about their meeting Jeanie did not bother to find out. She did not mention the meeting to Gregory and neither did he say anything about it.

But the path of jealousy is a tortuous one. She felt humiliated. She did not confront Gregory about his affair but her very silence caused an exaggeration of the unhappiness within her, beyond all reasonable proportions.

She relived the meeting with Miranda so many times each night that it eventually took all sorts of weird angles. In her mind she imagined Gregory telling the woman her most intimate weaknesses.

Like a repetition of the night in the restaurant shortly after they had met, when she had confided that she'd been masturbating. He would be leaning across the table, twirling Miranda's curls, while Jeanie turned red, imagining the two of them laughing at her expense.

She felt silly, thinking about that incident. Those were the days when she still worked quite hard at thinking up new angles of love making for her man and, in the knowledge that it would definitely excite him again, which it did, immediately, she could remember, she had brought his ear down to her mouth to whisper her stupidities into his ear.

She imagined him saying to Miranda, laughingly, 'You should have seen her face! Disgusted. Like she was looking at a snake – never having seen one before. And she's a midwife, believe it or not', exposing Jeanie's naiveté for a laugh, when he had brought home a five-fingered contraption within the first year of their marriage, which scratched her when he inserted it into her.

She'd ached for weeks after. No longer ashamed of not knowing, now angry and ashamed of the abuses the man had exposed her to, during her years of innocence and beyond, Jeanie dreamt her humiliations, implanting them in her mind, projecting them into disturbed sleep, during long lonely nights.

Lack of sleep, a fast-decreasing self-image, overeating, constant depression, missing Zogi, confusion as to whether or not to see her lawyer about a divorce and deciding to postpone it, just not knowing what to do – finally caught up with Jeanie.

Without knowing this, Jeanie's concentration at work was being affected. Usually extremely proud of her method of doing her job and the trust that she could feel coming from her mums, young and old, she had lately become thoughtless and unpunctual. Her readiness to be available to her patients, no matter how tired she felt, seemed to be something of the past.

The telephone became an enemy and she had to exercise strong control not to let her patients feel her irritability at, what she now unreasonably concluded, to be the unfair privilege which pregnant women and women with babies think they have over the time and efforts of others.

It came to a head when Jeanie was called out to deliver Mrs. Delany's seventh baby.

## Chapter 13

When the call came, Jeanie immediately went to the Delaney home.

Mrs. Delaney smiled weakly at Nurse Dean when her husband showed Jeanie into the bedroom where she was lying on her back, everything tidily prepared.

Even the little table in the corner of the room, usually cluttered with laundry or sewing, was now cleared and covered with a clean, white tablecloth which hung down to the floor, for the nurse to spread her instruments out on.

Jeanie hardly had time to put on her gloves when water started gushing out between Mrs. Delaney's large, bent legs.

'That was very well timed,' said Jeanie as she pulled Mrs. Delaney's night dress further up, putting her left arm under the lady's heavy body and lifting her slightly to adjust the tattered old towel which they had put under her, over the newspapers and plastic which were covering the sheet.

A massive contraction hit the woman's body, and with her worker's hands she gripped the top of the blanket, blue veins giving away her resistance as she tried to reflect the pain back into the earth where it had come from. Her hands were scared, calloused and arthritic.

Just as the nurse thought that the baby's head was about to come, she witnessed something which few midwives in all their years of practice ever see.

The umbilical cord came rushing out ahead of the baby in a gush of birth fluid!

Frantically the nurse tried to remember her training. What does one do in such a case? The umbilical cord is the baby's lifeline before it is born, before it is able to breathe for itself. Even if the head is out, the baby cannot yet breathe because the lungs are still airtight inside the mother's pelvis. What to do?

'Mrs. Delaney!' the nurse shouted, panic in her voice, knowing that the husband could hear from outside the door in the sitting room. He would know that things had suddenly turned bad.

Jeanie panicked. She pulled on the umbilical cord, knowing that it is only when the infant's chest is ejected that the lungs can expand and draw in the first breath of air. She prayed that the head would come, so the automatic suction could happen in the same way it does when one surfaces from underwater.

The cord would not move, and stretched tightly under Jeanie's hand. It was caught between pelvic bone and the infant's head and the life-giving oxygen was immediately cut off before the baby was born.

'Mr. Delaney!' the nurse now screamed, knowing he could hear. As her husband rushed into the room, Mrs. Delaney pressed down and the little dark head, wet and sticky, came out and crushed the umbilical call on the rim of the pelvic cavity.

'Stop pushing!' Jeanie pleaded, so she could get the head back to release the cord. She prayed for just enough time to make a space between little head and bone, so the cord could be pushed back into the woman's insides, for the little one to continue to get the oxygen which was being blocked off, oxygen which would keep it alive until the chest came out and it could take its first breath.

Jeanie gently applied pressure on the baby's head, with the fingers of her right hand extended widely, as with her palm she tried to push the little head back.

But Mrs. Delaney had stopped listening. She pushed with all her might and the little head slipped out and crunched the cord against the hard pelvic rim next to the baby's ear.

For the first time in her life Jeanie went into a blind panic.

She half lifted the poor woman up by her buttocks with her left hand, while at the same time still pushing against the infant's little head to release the now jammed cord. This did not help.

Her husband ran to her side and the woman, too, panicked, as she sensed the emergency. She bore down in a final, uncontrollable, unstoppable reflex. The veins in her neck and on her temples extended with her body's supreme effort to rid itself of the foreign body, whose nine months of tenancy inside its comfortable, liquid haven, had expired.

The woman gave one last heave, and, face turning red, pushed down. Nature had taken over and she could not possibly now be stopped. In horror the nurse watched the infant being pushed forward, head coming out fully and shoulders securely catching the cord in another inextricable grip, cutting off the last bit of oxygen which might still have kept the baby alive.

The nurse had to postpone her feelings of horror and complete helplessness. She went through the final mechanics of birth, knowing that the baby had not taken a breath and would never do so.

She kept her shame till later, when she realised that Mr. Delaney had seen the final, pitiful scene as she gently helped the limp little body out of its mother's body, plump little feet slipping out last.

Although she knew by then that it was too late, she worked very fast. She put her thumb and little finger around the outside of the baby's legs, middle fingers between, suspending the infant upside down. It dangled there listlessly, limp like a small dead rabbit, upside down, without a sound. The nurse cleaned its face; lay it down again, face up between the mother's still bent legs.

She did not look up, did not meet the father's eyes as, knowing it was too late, she put her hands on either side of the little chest and applied pressure in rhythmic movements, while covering the baby's mouth and nose with her mouth, forcing her breath into its little chest, which rose and fell in physiological obedience.

With all her intellect she tried to force the little infant to start breathing. But she was forced to stop, to do some explaining, for it was futile.

Nurse Dean finally gave up and slowly lifted her head, looking right into the puzzled, unassuming eyes of Mr. Delaney, who was still silently waiting at the foot of the bed, not having said a word. His face bore sadness and defeat.

What a perfect birth this would otherwise have been, her thoughts accused her, as she lowered her head, and with precision completed the birth process. She delivered the placenta by applying the slightest of pressures on the woman's abdomen.

Mrs. Delaney, knowing without being told what had happened, was lying on her back dejectedly, large thighs still widespread, eyes closed, tears running down past her dishevelled hair into the equally untidy pillow.

The suddenness of a stillbirth, caused by whatever reason, is one of the hardest things for a midwife to explain to parents. The next ten minutes were the most difficult Jeanie Dean had ever had to live through.

Stuttering, struggling for the right words, she tried to explain to the distraught couple the mysterious twist which nature had played on them.

The fact that the dear, good people made no accusation, and did not question their midwife's abilities in any way, did not help to make Nurse Dean feel any better. She felt inept and incompetent.

She questioned the better judgement of the universe, yet grudgingly admired its direct aim in hitting its objects with their misfortune. While giving recognition to its precise timing and apparent, ironic, consideration of particular circumstance - in this case the poverty of the Delaney family – Jeanie could not help but blame herself, as if the outcome were at all within her control. It gave her no consolation to admit that the Delaneys were materially better off without a further burden on their meagre finances.

What happened in the Delaney home after she tiredly left, she was never to know.

The experience, however, was a turning point for her.

## Chapter 14

Jeanie made a snap decision as she left the unhappy couple behind to face their world.

She still did not know what to do about her marriage. Her life, seemingly determined not yet to reverse its steady downward slide, was for a long time yet to put her through trials which she could not have imagined in her worst nightmares.

Without bothering to go home, Jeanie drove straight to the head office of Matron Simon.

Sitting outside the office on a hard bench, placed, it seemed, where it was destined to increase nervousness and discomfort, Jeanie got her first opportunity to rehearse her story. She discarded the idea to say that there was an illness or death in the family. This might cause problems at a later stage, although she did not think that Matron Simon – such a stiff personification of authority – was at all interested in the family affairs of her staff.

Jeanie made up a story in her head, of having to accompany her husband on a business trip. This restored some of her self-esteem and feeling of importance. She would tell matron that her husband had thought she had known about it and had asked her to organise her time to fit in with his trip.

She knew that there was a full complement of staff on duty at that time, because everybody was waiting for the summer before taking their holidays, and she suspected there would not be a problem for her to be able to take a week or so off.

But the 'Yes, what can we do for you, nurse' of Matron Simon in her usually frosty Scottish accent, emptied Jeanie's mind of her prepared excuse. She felt as if she were suddenly falling into a well. The whole trauma of the afternoon had, without her knowing it, let her tired body speak for her.

'I am extremely exhausted, Matron. I need to rest,' adding, expecting not to be believed without a better reason, 'also, I have to – '

'Do you want to take some time off?' Matron sarcastically interrupted her, eyes down, re-arranging an already tidy desk, and Jeanie had the chance to swallow down the words which were perching on her tongue - that her marriage was in a mess.

Jeanie grabbed the opening offered her by the matron's disinterest in her personal affairs. She nodded, 'Yes, please Matron. Are you able to arrange for someone to stand in for me please?'

'That can be arranged,' Obviously Matron Simon had other things on her mind, and she wanted Jeanie out of her office. She stood up, and at the moment the telephone rang.

As she reached for it, she said, 'Go and sort it out with Sister Jones. She'll re-arrange the roster,' and Jeanie was out of the office like a shot, through the inter-leading door into Sister Jones' office.

The arrangements were quickly made and, within thirty minutes Jeanie was driving back to her home, relieved that the first part of her plan had gone so well. But her heart was racing. She expected things to go wrong, because a big decision like the one she was about to make could not go smoothly. Of this she was convinced.

First: Hand the government Anglia back. Second: Hire a cheap car until she gets back to work.

She drove home from Rent a Jallopie in a tiny yellow rented Volkswagen feeling lighter, and threw some clothes into a suitcase with much anxiety. If Gregory should walk into the house while she was there it would be almost impossible to explain herself out of this one and a fight would be inevitable.

She did not bother to leave a note for him.

Feeling free and excited as she turned out of their road onto the main street, Jeanie headed straight for the bank to draw money, then filled up the car, checked tyre pressure, oil and water levels and headed straight out onto the N1 from Bellville, starting the one and a half thousand-kilometre journey to Johannesburg.

She wanted to get to Hillbrow. Why, she could not exactly say, except that she knew some comrades there who might be able to tell her where Zogi was. All else failing, she would contact Zogi's parents, but this she dreaded, in case they had also not heard from Zogi.

The drive through the Paarl mountains was comforting. Jeanie stopped the car on one of the hills and got out to stretch her legs, possessively enjoying the beauty of her country.

With all its problems of racial discrimination and class distinctions, there was no other place in the world where she would rather be. Jeanie felt soothed by the mountains lying in the distance all around her, in the same way that the grape vines were soothed as they stood silently satisfied in the valleys, throwing up their greens and darkest of browns to the sun.

At Worcester she stopped off, where her father's family lived. During the nineteen seventies, when apartheid was still at its peak, there were no hotels, motels or any kind of rest room facilities available for non-white travellers on the extensive national roads in South Africa. Jeanie knew that once she passed through Worcester and entered the Klein Karoo, the small semi-desert which stretches for miles, she would be unable to find anywhere to sleep that night.

She drove off the N1 freeway and decided to stop at a service station to fill up with fuel before going through the town to the suburbs where her family lived.

The hospitality of the people in the Cape was part of Jeanie's genetic goodwill. Her old aunt, with hardly any room to spare in her house with seven children, was very glad to see her. They spent happy hours that night, comparing experiences on how life had changed. Her cousin, also called Jeanie, and a few months older, sat up with her late into the night, laughing at the many stories which Jeanie told her about her work.

She really needed the warmth and friendliness of her lovely people. How glad she was that it is customary for families to just drop by, without forewarning or reprimand. They fussed over her and made her feel wanted, important and loved.

Almost the whole family, except for the elder brother who was working night shift, were up at five the next morning to see her off. Jeanie, after being served a big bowl of mieliepap (maize porridge), drove away, with promises to call and see them soon. And, of course, to write regularly.

The hugs they gave her were just what she'd needed, she thought as she later stopped to have a cup of warm, strong, sweet coffee from the flask which her aunt had given her.

The extreme cold of the night started to turn into what promised to be a blisteringly hot day as Jeanie saw the sky turn pink with the rising sun over the hills. She had heard it said that the Karoo actually got snow in the winter, but she had never seen that, and the heat of the early winter morning made that hard to believe.

All she saw now, driving along the straight road which stretches on as far as the eye could see over the flat land, was the openness of the veld, hardly any trees visible, except for the occasional Acacia in the distance, with roots deep in the earth hunting for water, standing firmly against the winds which sweep across the lowlands where scrub lies as low as in the Yorkshire moors. Not enough rains had come to relieve the devastation of the summer. The little starlings nesting in the thorns of the Acacia trees were only too grateful for a place to tend their young, for there were no other trees available.

After hours of steady driving, Jeanie turned in at the Three Sisters, three koppies, or hills, which stand with life-like breasts and upright nipples silhouetted against the blue sky.

The little Anglia sighed in satisfaction before its engine went quiet after Jeanie had filled up and parked the car next to the only restaurant in the small town. She was barred from entry, not this time by a written sign, but by a common knowledge of the law.

Her heart started racing while standing outside the little window which served as the shopping section for blacks on the side of the supermarket. She looked through the big glass windows at the whites doing their shopping in air-conditioned comfort and stood waiting with mounting discomfort.

Jeanie desperately needed to use a toilet.

Obviously, time for another confrontation, which would, as always, be sweet in its aftermath. But the wilfulness needed to go through with it always takes much more courage than the action deserves. But then, Jeanie was used to confrontation. Was she not a Capetonian, renowned for their premeditated defiance of the law?

Ladies – Whites only, the sign shouted out its warning as she walked under it through the entrance into the rest room around the corner.

How beautiful it was inside! Rows of spotlessly white hand basins lined the walls, which were covered with a pastel green wallpaper. Jeanie purposefully walked across the thick, floral-patterned carpet of the entrance room with its comfortable, imported Parker Knoll chairs nestling next to a low dressing table in the corner. She smiled at her reflection in the floor-to-ceiling mirrors. Past them she walked, into one of the toilets.

Nobody else was in there. All was quiet.

She locked the toilet door and sat down, thinking all they can do is to tell me to get out, which I'm going to do, anyway. Her bladder emptied itself with almost painful relief - when her feeling of satisfaction was shattered.

The outer door opened with a bang and a woman's voice, in the flat Afrikaans of the Karoo, said loudly, '*Die meid is innie toilet, baas!*' (the servant girl is in the toilet, boss!)

Heart now pounding, Jeanie unconsciously moved on the toilet seat, unable to stop the flow of urine, trying to make it fall against the side of the toilet bowl so that it would not be heard.

'Come out!' a man's deep voice belted out in Afrikaans.

Silence, while Jeanie slowly let out the last bit, relief postponing fear. Then, with deliberate slowness, while her mind was turning over fast, not sure what to do next, she did what women have to do after raising herself from the toilet seat. She took her time. Then she carefully opened the door, half expecting the man to be standing in front of her.

The short, flat-faced Afrikaner was standing in the doorway at the far end of the room. A thin, tiny, yellow-skinned woman with short, dry, sun-bleached and equally yellow hair, was standing behind the man, half hiding from Jeanie and staring past her boss' stocky frame at Jeanie with comically accusing eyes.

'You know you're breaking the law, hey?' he said in Afrikaans, arms akimbo.

Jeanie ignored him completely and, holding her head high, wishing that her nose was just a bit sharp for ultimate effect, she strutted across the room, staring into the face of the Afrikaner as she walked past them.

He must have been caught by surprise. She turned her head and flashed a bright smile of contempt at him. His face went red. It looked as if he was about to lose control. But Jeanie by this time had her back to him, watching him in the big mirror while washing her hands. He watched her, at a loss for anything sensible to say.

Then he weakly shouted at her back, 'See it doesn't happen again!' and stormed out.

You've got a hope in hell that I'll ever come here again, she thought, still not having said a word. She stared at his back in the mirror, then turned around and threw a pitying stare at the young domestic servant who was still standing at the door, mouth open in her pretty light brown face, light brown eyes, flat and opening up from the almost non-existent bridge of a nose, wide in shocked surprise at the cheek of this strange woman.

I hope she has learnt something today, Jeanie thought as she started the car up again and turned back onto the freeway, refusing to queue up at the little side window for a cool drink despite her need for something cold, so avoiding further humiliation.

A slight wind had come up. Jeanie drove slower so as not to miss the beauty of her surroundings. Her sense of belonging deepened at the familiar sight of light blobs of fine weeds, little round balloons, being driven across the veld, spreading their pollen in readiness for germination in the spring.

She stopped off again as evening approached, when she had driven through the Klein Karoo, past Kimberley. At Bloemfontein she filled up with fuel again and stretched her legs by the roadside, to finish the last few bites of her packed lunch and cold tea. The yellow and white daizies and vygies were already popping their heads out all over the veld and, although she could not see it, Jeanie could hear the loud croak of a bull frog, probably announcing a precious discovery of water, shouting out, as if in warning to the stone crickets to stop attracting attention with their high-pitched screeching. Turtle doves, hiding somewhere, were coo-cooing their 'I love you too' into the still early evening, relaxing her tired muscles.

As night settled in Jeanie could feel her eyes getting tired, but she was on a sharp lookout for the zebra, antelopes, wildebeest, ostriches and karakul (lynx) through whose area she was passing. She had to put her foot down sharply on the brakes as a group of springbok rushed across the road, springing along, front feet together and back legs slightly spread, jumping their way past her life.

She arrived in Hillbrow six hours later, well into the night.

## Chapter 15

Whilst the rest of South Africa was sleeping in its separateness, it also offered 'international' accommodation to those who could afford it, in mixed-race hotels. Jeanie headed for one of those.

She knew that the law expected her to prove that she was a black foreign national to enjoy international status, but she was going to take a chance, knowing that the reception desks were usually staffed by her own people and that they would probably look the other way.

Which is exactly what the lovely young lady with her big smile at the hotel in Pretoria Street did. Jeanie parked her car, booked in, dropped her bag and postponed her tiredness.

Zogi must be somewhere close by. She used the public telephone in the entrance hall of the hotel. She phoned a friend of theirs in Soweto. Queeny's was open all hours. But nobody answered the phone.

At a loss for what to do next, Jeanie went upstairs and fell into a dreamless sleep. Early the next morning she headed straight to Soweto to see Queeny.

'She arrived here, about three months ago, with a man. I don't know him, and I don't like him,' said Queeny, so called because she was a shebeen queen, sitting open legged, pulling up her wide skirt. Although it was still early morning, she had some customers there and she was pouring beers into large mugs. Her boyfriend, half her age and as thin as she was overweight, trotted between sitting room and kitchen serving the liquor.

Jeanie awkwardly stood in the corner, feeling unsure of herself. 'How's she?' she asked anxiously.

'Yo. I don't know what's wrong with that girl. She's got everything going for her, but she wants to be involved with these rotten people,' was all Jeanie could get out of Queeny, whom she left to her illegal business.

Jeanie combed the streets of Soweto for two days trying to find Zogi. She was sent from one house to another by sympathetic, but disinterested contacts. Because she did not carry a pass which meant she could not legally be in the township at night, Jeanie did this during the day, returning to her hotel in the evening.

Groups of idle young people were hanging around in the area, especially in front of shop corners, with nothing to do but contemplate their unemployment and frustration. How can they be labelled as lazy, she wondered, when there is no work for them and no social security to help them along their way?

Jeanie felt no fear in the black areas. The coloured people in South Africa, having always been told that they are not black, generally enjoy a much better standard of living. Jeanie was grateful that she had been allowed to wake up to the hidden truths behind apartheid, whilst many of her peers and family still regarded themselves, without question, as white appendages and took their privileges of being classified coloured for granted.

It struck her that once apartheid was dismantled the real teaching would start. The results of apartheid, the prejudices which developed between the people themselves, will have to be reversed and new ideas born, before a new way of life could be contemplated. This insight her political awakening had given her.

Driving through the streets of Pimville, Jeanie compared the conditions of the location, as the black townships were called, to her own, coloured, town and the beauty and orderliness of the white areas she passed by on her way back into Johannesburg.

She passed Triomf, so named because of the literal triumph of the whites over the people who used to live there. After years of bulldozing the shacks of the blacks who had been living there for centuries, they had eventually taken the town, after successfully carting lorry loads of resistant families with their meagre belongings out of the place of their birth.

Sophiatown, it used to be called, in the nineteen-fifties, alive with music and laughter, the birthplace of many a jazz musician.

Now quiet, clean, white and sterilized, the only black person to be seen was the occasional domestic servant, called a boy who, with old black hands and tired eyes, served the whites in their single storied sanitized houses.

What inequality.

The immaculately laid out lawns and playing fields and upmarket architecture of the beautiful houses in Triomf on her left stood out in luxurious vulgarity against the little box-like houses on the other side of the fields. Row upon identical row, behind flimsy wire net fences in dusty, grey streets with no visible street lighting, the houses on the other side, in Soweto, waited as if in a brief pause before taking off in the strong wind which threatened to lift them up at any time. Most schools, almost all of them without playing fields or windows, ready to be condemned.

Comparing the ugliness with trying to learn strange facts of histories in Europe completely removed from their surroundings, in an alien language called Afrikaans, the young people were soon to attack the structures of their frustration, burning the schools down, to the criticism of the rest of the western world, who could never understand their powerlessness.

Eventually Jeanie was forced to call on Zogi's parents.

# Chapter 16

The day Jeanie decided to go and see Dr. and Mrs. Pillay, was also the day when things had gone frighteningly wrong in the Pillay family.

Zogi's parents were both famous lawyers. The husband and wife team were well respected in the liberation community, for they were outspoken activists, internationally known for their commitment to the struggle for freedom.

Jeanie had never met them. In fact, she was feeling rather timid when she knocked on the white door in the quiet suburb of Johnnesburg where they lived.

All was quiet, nobody answered the door.

Deciding not to leave it there, Jeanie went straight to their offices in downtown Jo'burg.

When she walked around the corner into the road where their offices were, Jeanie sensed that something big had happened.

The street was full of people, milling about, restless, talking with each other in Sotho. Jeanie could not speak any African language. It was a great sadness to her, well into her later years, to have to admit that she could not understand when spoken to with impatience by blacks who expected her to respond, because they all looked like family.

Apartheid had made sure that Jeanie's people were kept away from other ethnic African black groups like the

Zulus and, in Cape Town where Jeanie came from, the AmaXhosa.

And now, here in Johannesburg, she equally could not understand what was being said in Sotho, because she had never had the opportunity to mix with her black brothers and sisters at school or socially, had not been allowed to even go into the residential areas where they lived, without a permit, which she never could acquire.

Jeanie stood watching the crowd, not knowing what to do. Eventually she plucked up courage and approached a tired old man on the street.

''Molo uncle,' she greeted. He responded in a language unknown to her, raising his eyes at her when she did not answer his question.

'You don't speak my language?!' his half question, half accusation made her cheeks sting in shame.

'Sorry uncle,' Jeanie said quietly, dropping her head.

The old man smiled, a kindly smile, nodded his head and continued to speak with her in very good English.

'It's not our fault, I know, my girl. But what can an old man do for you, pretty one?'

'What's happened here today?' she asked.

'Why do you want to know?' he hit back, suspicion now clouding his eyes. 'I'm a close friend of Dr. Pillay's daughter, Zogi and I want to speak with Dr. and Mrs. Pillay, but …'

'Ah, yes,' he said, looking her up and down. 'What do you know about Dr. Pillay?' Just a security check to make sure that she was not an informer trying to sniff out information.

'I have been friends with Zogi, their daughter for a long time,' Jeanie explained. 'We both live in Cape Town. I know that Dr. Pillay has been ill lately, and I heard that a few weeks ago, when the rally was cancelled in Johannesburg, he was attacked in his car on the way home. I heard that he had landed up in hospital and I don't know how he is now.'

This seemed to satisfy the old gentleman, for the news about Dr. Pillay was not known to people outside the struggle, for it had never been reported in the news.

'Sad news, very sad news today,' he said, and Jeanie's heart sank.

'We believe that he was killed last night. A bomb went off in their office on the other side of this building,' he said, pointing across the road where the crowds were milling about. 'We are waiting for news.'

'Oh my God!' Jeanie said, close to tears. 'Oh my God!' she said again, gasping into her fear.

'Do you know where Mrs. Pillay and their daughter are?' Jeanie asked in a frightened voice.

'Did you not know that they have both been in detention for the past few months?'

'Oh Lord!' Jeanie gasped again, as tears started out of her eyes. The kind man took her hand and led her away from the crowd, where he stopped under a tree with her.

'We have not heard about Mrs. Pillay, where she is being held, how she is. This will be a great shock for her. Her daughter was released not too long ago, a few weeks ago, I heard, but I don't know where she is now.' So that is why Zogi had not been in touch!

The news of Dr. Pillay's death shook Jeanie to the core. It appeared in the newspapers that night, well after Jeanie had found Zogi in a place which she would never have wanted to find her worst enemy.

# Chapter 17

She eventually got a lead from one of the comrades she knew at the local Catholic church in Pimville.

'She's somewhere in Hillbrow, I think,' he said. 'I met her in the street two weeks ago and she said she was living in Quartz Street, I think at the Hoffman New Yorker.'

Zogi was not at the Hoffman New Yorker. Nobody knew her there.

The urge to see her friend again became entwined with an increasing despair, which became more tangible as she walked down Pretoria Street in Hillbrow.

Walking east from Klein Street, Jeanie went into every pub and popped in at every amusement room, billiard hall, snooker room. She even checked out sordid little hotels where she knew a room could be rented for a few rands an hour, where the street girls hung out.

On the corner of Quartz Street Jeanie saw one of the girls, whose skimpy black leather shorts pulled up between succulent buttocks, fish net stockings covering her long legs, half of her exposed breasts falling forward flauntingly as she bent down to speak to a curb crawler with leering eyes.

Hillbrow depressed her.

In Claim Street she saw the suffering of the street children, Twilight Kids as they were called because they live on the streets and are always in a glue-sniffing twilight of their own.

A group of about five of them was sitting at the entrance to the alley between Woolworths and the Pizza Hut. Bare footed, their feet looked like old car tyres, rough and torn, marked with scars.

The group ranged between ages five and thirteen. They sat huddled up together. Every now and then one of them would grip the right cuff of the sleeve of the tattered adult jacket he was wearing, and sniff down into it, his eyes rolling back from the fumes, which Jeanie knew probably came from glue or petrol.

One of the children looked up at her and waves of shock went through her system. He must be only about 12, she thought, looking at his body, as thin as a reed inside the outsized overcoat he was wearing. But his face was that of a very old man, wrinkles on his forehead and down the sides of his face, his course skin tightly drawn across hollow cheeks, pulling into folds and puckered up in places like that of a wise old lizard. His mouth, which was open as he screwed up his blank eyes to squint up at her, was drawn in a permanent smirk. His unnaturally small, egg-shaped head jumped from side to side in the nervous jerks of a shell-shocked war veteran.

Sickened and angry, Jeanie's eyes moved to three old ladies sitting drinking tea on the pavement opposite the group of hungry children, their diamonds glittering in the setting sun. Jeanie caught a part of their conversation '...belong in their own areas,' and she wanted to shout out her anger at the unfairness of her society.

But then she also realised that Hillbrow was probably the only place in South Africa where the street children could survive, for there they at least had a chance of a return on their begging. Whereas, in townships and rural areas, they would simply starve to death.

Hillbrow, one of the only places in South Africa in those years where white and black lived side by side, in the flats and surrounding houses. Hillbrow with its hotels, where the Group Areas Act had been ignored for decades, mothering, mixing and nurturing, without distinction or recrimination, nationals and foreigners of all colours and means. Hillbrow, the cosmopolitan thorn in the festering flesh of apartheid.

She took a slow walk back to the Mariston Hotel in Claim Street where she had taken a furnished apartment for a week, to the luxury enjoyed by those who have the money to live comfortably and, once again, was grateful that she, at least, had had a bit of luck and education, and was able to afford some of the comforts South Africa so grudgingly protected for the small minority.

Jeanie did, eventually find her friend.

## Chapter 18

It happened by pure co-incidence.

Tired and by now convinced of the apparent hopelessness of her task, Jeanie was sitting on the patio of a little hotel, sipping an orange drink. Exhausted and not able to think of what to do next, she was staring over the railing onto the continuous stream of traffic and people milling around on the corner of Pretoria Street and Catherine Avenue.

Suddenly she saw a familiar head from the top, looking down. She was sure it was Zogi. Same long brown hair, leaning on the arm of a very thin man in black leather jacket and skintight leather trousers, which hardly covered the bundle of bones inside it.

But before Jeanie had made a move, they had disappeared around the corner of Catherine Avenue.

Jeanie ran down the steps onto the pavement, around the corner, just as they were going into a dark doorway on the other side of the street.

Impatiently she waited for the traffic light to stop the steady flow of traffic so that she could run across the street, bumping into people, pushing them aside in her haste.

The stench of urine was overpowering as she passed from the flashing neon signs of the street into the dark passageway. She felt nauseous. Cockroaches scampered away from her as she crossed the gloomy quadrangle between the back of the blocks of flats to get to the rickety flight of steps which acted as the fire escape.

But they had disappeared.

Just as she decided to go up the staircase anyway, in the hope that they might still be in one of the passages, a man appeared from behind a six-foot drum, from a door which she had not seen.

'You must be looking for the third floor,' he said, without asking her what she wanted, before he walked out onto the street.

Not knowing what the third floor was about, Jeanie climbed up the staircase. The passage there was dimly lit and it took her a while to adjust her eyes to the darkness.

Then she saw the only open door on the other of the passage. The noise which came from inside was deafening. As was the stench.

As she walked through the door it banged shut behind her and, for a brief second, she stood behind it, waiting to be told to leave. But nobody took any notice of her and she realised that being black had its advantages, for nobody even bothered to question why she was there.

She immediately saw the frail, fine face of her friend. Zogi was sitting, squashed between two other people on a couch, head bent slightly forward, eyes half closed, as if she were dreaming.

As Jeanie watched her, Zogi's arm moved up to her mouth in a circular movement.

'Zogi', Jeanie half whispered, in absolute concentration trying to convince her friend not to do it, even as Zogi put the pipe to her mouth. She took a long, satisfying draw, leaning back into the curved arm behind her head, about to close her eyes and lean back into the ecstasy of whatever it was she had inhaled into her fragile lungs.

The whisper did reach Zogi's befuddled brain, for she turned her head towards her friend and, slowly, Jeanie's face floated through her mind, and flashed back into her eyes, which opened in surprise, resting on Jeanie's face.

But even as Jeanie thought Zogi had recognised her, the girl closed her eyes once again and, her head flopping to the side, she slipped back into the darkness of insensibility.

Jeanie rushed over and bent in front of her friend, folding up her extended feet at the knees so as to come closer to her. Not conscious of anyone else, Jeanie leaned forward and brought Zogi's flopping head to face her.

The eyes opened again and, this time, they were unable to avoid the pure will and domination which penetrated into them from Jeanie's determined brown eyes.

Zogi had recognised her.

'Hello Jeanie,' she said in a tired voice, from between clenched teeth, little drops of white spittle forced out onto tight, drawn lips. She tried to smile, but her face could not support the effort. Instead, her mouth drew down into a little girl grimace and big tears scorched their way down her hot cheeks.

Jeanie took Zogi's face between her palms, making it impossible for the girl to turn her head away.

'I've come to fetch you, Zogi,' Jeanie said softly to her friend, afraid that the brief connection might disappear.

Zogi looked at Jeanie listlessly, her head heavy in Jeanie's open hands, crying softly, not able to say a word.

Jeanie forgot manners and stood up impulsively, then plonked herself down between Zogi and the man sitting on her left, squeezing her bottom between them. She lifted his arm off the back of the settee as she sat down, not looking at him, not daring to take her eyes off her friend's face.

The man jumped up out of the seat and out of his dreamland. Jeanie was later to get to know him, and like him, as a refined, well-mannered person.

'What's wrong with you, lady,' he said in an effeminate voice, dusting his thighs in confusion as he turned his back to them and casually strolled out of the room.

Jeanie did not watch him leave, for her body had gone stiff in a further shock. As she sat down next to Zogi, her eyes wondered down onto her friend's body for the first time. Below the large, brown tunic Zogi was wearing Jeanie saw an unfortunate bulge.

Zogi was well into pregnancy.

Jeanie's first reaction was one of complete and utter sorrow. She had to steel herself not to break into tears. Her throat constricted and her chest pressed all air out of her lungs as she hung onto self-control.

## Chapter 19

Jeanie's extended right arm, now around Zogi's shoulders, pulled the emaciated shoulders closer to her and she put her head on Zogi's chest bone, her face down, taking up the limited space between Zogi's small breasts, filled up in later pregnancy. The high, rounded top of Zogi's abdomen, warm and rich, pulsated under Jeanie's ear as she made deep contact with the insides of her friend.

They sat like that for a few moments in an intimacy which very seldom is repeated in a single lifetime. Karma took its timely circle as the warmth and love which this very friend of hers had given to Jeanie so unselfishly, flowed back to her, a hundred fold multiplied.

Jeanie's old aunt in Worcester would have stood proud had she known that the kindness and understanding which she had lent to Jeanie in such abundance was now flowing, unhindered, through her into an unknown, much more needy person.

In the completeness of the moment Jeanie's main purpose on earth was there for all, but herself, to see. Jeanie's life was destined to be a passage for non-discriminatory love. And her aim, also unknown to her, was to stay empty so as always to be available to be filled up so that love could always pass through her to others.

Jeanie was yet to learn that when she served her life purpose, as an avenue between the source of compassion and its waiting objects, as she was doing in that moment, that the very naturalness and effortlessness of her actions would make her feel as she felt now, complete and, strangely, satisfied.

Trading time must have been over then, for their reverie was interrupted by a loud voice shouting 'Ok then, people, let's start moving.' Jeanie opened her eyes and lifted her head to see that Zogi had also heard this, for she struggled to lift herself from her seat.

The freshness of the night outside was just what the two girls needed. Jeanie decided not to call for a taxi, but to walk back to the hotel with Zogi, who seemed to have recovered enough to keep in step with her, Jeanie's stronger body giving her the support she needed to stay upright.

Claim Street is a steep downhill from Hillbrow and it was not difficult for them to reach Jeanie's hotel, about five hundred metres down the hill.

In her little apartment Jeanie put Zogi to bed and sat with her friend. They had not said anything to each other after Zogi's 'Hello, Jeanie' earlier. Like a zombi, Zogi had allowed Jeanie to take the shoes off her pigeon-toed feet and swing her legs onto the bed.

Now covered with a light blanket she lay on the bed, back in the security of her dreams.

Jeanie sat for a long time holding her friend's hand, just looking at her and sending out all the love she could to her unconscious friend. She thought of the times when Zogi had acted as her protector from attack, defender from misunderstanding.

She remembered the day after her last detention when Zogi had been there to feel and cry with. She recalled all the times Zogi had sat through her endless complaining, without comment, acting as her sounding board.

Jeanie talked quietly to her sleeping friend as to a baby, loving her, until she, too, fell asleep.

She did get the holiday which she had longed for when she left Cape Town without plans.

The next week was packed with fun and laughter.

The weather had become warm and promising and Jeanie and Zogi spent hours lazing in the sun on deckchairs and towels at the hotel's private swimming pool. Sipping iced lemonades in long glasses with ice cream sundaes and occasionally ordering a cold beer shandy from a waiter who, with the white shirt, black trousers and bow tied uniform of his trade, made them feel like real ladies of leisure.

Jeanie splashed in the water and even Zogi, forgetting her awkward body, sat on the side, cooling her feet, every now and then dipping in.

Then they had a picnic on the grass at the lake at Johannesburg's musical fountain, watching the different sized arcs of water being spiralled 12 metres up into the sky.

The heavy drums of Beethoven's 5th brought on wild showers in waterfalls of psychedelic colour as the violins manoeuvred bows of water, in streaks as thin as their strings, and Jeanie dreamed that Zogi would play her violin again.

They strolled through the zoo holding hands, eating almost all the nuts they had bought for the monkeys. Lazy hours were spent walking through the many parks laid out all over the city, offering money hunters relief from its dirt and grime.

Then they took a slow drive to Pretoria's lake, making jokes about the serious white clerks rushing around this legislative city where the evil laws of the land were made.

But they said nothing about their plans. It was as if Jeanie and Zogi had arrived at an unexpressed pact not to spoil their time together by talking about the uncertainty of their futures. They were afraid that voicing their fears might make them bigger.

Sitting on the balcony at Café de Paris in the cool of the late evening, the subject was brought up by Jeanie.

'Zogi, I have to leave on Sunday. How about coming back to Cape Town with me?'

Zogi's face went sad as she looked at her friend. 'I can't, Jeanie. I have this problem.'

'You know that's nonsense. You are as much on drugs as I am,' thinking she was talking about her dope smoking.

'No, it's not that,' said Zogi simply. Then she cried, there on the pavement, she sobbed the tears which Jeanie had expected all the time, but which had not come. Jeanie sat and looked at her small friend whose head was bent, whose sorrow was shaded by her long brown hair which fell forward to give her relief from the stares of passersby.

'I don't know where my mum is, Jeanie,' Zogi looked up at Jeanie with red eyes and runny nose. 'I blocked out my dad's death and have not been back to the house at all …'

## Chapter 20

It was only later that night that Jeanie realised how difficult things had been for her younger friend.

She did not know that Zogi, too, like herself, had actually been a runner for the underground movement, bringing back money over the borders from Botswana and Lesotho into South Africa to fund the movement.

She was amazed that her young friend Zogi had also been delivering pamphlets, holding meetings, handing out food, hiring halls.

It showed the success of the underground's policy of secrecy: Even close friends did not share between each other, so that the security police could learn nothing from others about what was happening with you under interrogation.

Zogi's work for the liberation movement was much harder than the community work which Jeanie was involved in, and she could not believe the stories which Zogi told her.

'The night before my father got killed, I had delivered two suitcases to his offices. They found the money and the books. I don't know how much was in there, I just went and left the cases when I got back from Botswana, before I went to the room I was renting.'

How her father had been killed would never really be known, like so many other deaths which went unsolved. What they were sure of was that the security police had

had a hand in it. They knew that the liberation activists were blamed for all the bombings which were happening in the country in protest against the suffering which apartheid was causing. What the world did not know was that the security police were planting many of the bombs themselves, while the world shook its head and condemned the violence of the people.

'I could not face my mother now, even if I knew where she was. I did not go to my father's funeral, which was held the very next day. I'm in a mess, Jeanie,' Zogi sobbed that night in the arms of her friend.

And then there was the pregnancy. Zogi did not say who the father was, and Jeanie did not ask. 'I cannot now face my mother with this pregnancy, if I get to see her again, which I doubt,' Zogi said, and Jeanie had no words of comfort for her. 'Here, in Jo'burg, I at least have a few people I can talk to, who accept me without judgment. I couldn't possibly go through the drama which I know will happen when my mum or my aunts see me. I cannot face them.'

'Why not come to Cape Town with me? It's time for me to leave Gregory. You and I know that. We could set up in a flat together and I will be there to help look after baby.'

The idea was a great one and the two of them dreamt of how great it would be. In their dream, and because it could only be a dream, they ignored the reality of how to find a place, for 'finding a flat' was but a figure of speech in cities where independent living could not happen unless you were a young white person.

It did happen that white people helped blacks to rent rooms or apartments in white areas by signing the contracts for them and charging a lot of money to do that, but Jeanie and Zogi knew of nobody who would take that risk for them. So, their idea of independent living, with a baby, could only be but a dream. They knew this.

They knew that their dreams were unable to pierce the combined force of religion, culture, society and economic dependency. Their dreams could only be dreams.

The subject was not brought up again and both of them, in their own way and in an effort not to worry the other, acted as if it had never been brought up. But the discomfort was there, and the happiness of the next day was marred by the knowledge that they were soon to part.

Jeanie did meet Zogi's boyfriend, whom, she discovered, was gay, a caring, loving person. She was pleased that Zogi was living with someone who was sensitive and kind. He jokingly talked about 'our' baby, although Jeanie knew that he was not the man who got Zogi pregnant.

She did not ask. The problems which Zogi had to face were too great for her to try to solve and she had her own life to go back to.

The threads which life was weaving were too intricate for them to unravel.

But Jeanie felt uplifted. She left Johannesburg feeling much better than when she had arrived. Zogi had promised to be in touch, and this was enough for her. She felt better, now that she knew that Zogi had not deserted her. Their love for each other had grown during their time apart. She appreciated the fact that Zogi had been prepared to spend the week with her so willingly, as if she were the only person in Zogi's life.

But the trip had not magically cleared away Jeanie's problems. Her statement that she was leaving Gregory, said on an impulse, now sounded empty. She had no idea how to leave him nor what to do should she even try. The old doubts about herself made her helpless to make the changes she needed so desperately to make in her own life.

Everything seemed too big. How could she even think of moving her stuff out, books, clothing, furniture? Gregory would not just stand there and watch her pack up and go. He would attack her again. And she would, as she had done so many times before, give in again and stay with him.

He might get violent. Or become emotional, which was even worse. 'You know I can't live without you, we've been together for so long and we do love each, don't we Jeanie, no matter what problems we might have. I promise I will never lift my hand to you again…We are not getting any younger and need each other…'

She could hear him in her head and already she was giving in, especially when he came to blackmail her about their vows, scaring her by reminding her about her religious and cultural responsibilities. 'We were honest when we took our vows,' he would say. 'No matter how things go, we hold our vows sacred. Divorce might be for other people, not for us. We have our beliefs. We are different.'

Also, leaving her home meant leaving her comforts, where she at least knew the rent was paid and she had no lack for money. The worry of having to survive on her own income was something which she had not even started to think about.

The problems hung as a web around her and she felt that if she even tried to shift position she would be entangled and strangled.

Divorce was out of the question. She felt trapped.

## Chapter 21

Jeanie's frustrations flooded her more as she neared Cape Town. When she had left, she had not known where she was going. Now, returning, she did not know where she was going next. She was afraid to go home.

As she had another day's leave left before having to report back on duty, she was reluctant to go straight home, wanting to postpone the problems she would face there for as long as possible.

Her bank account had by now been emptied and she could not afford to book into an hotel.

The only alternative was to find a friend to take her in for a day or two.

She phoned Sally and Bill. She got on ok with Bill, although she did not really like his wife. It happened to be the right time to go to them, though, as Bill said that his wife was away on a week's holiday and sure, Jeanie was welcome.

'You can't get yourself over this one, Jeanie,' her friend said that night over coffee. 'Gregory has already phoned here to ask if you are here. I'm sure he'll be popping around because he knows that you might come to us.'

Jeanie had already realised this. She had, by now, let go completely and had decided not to try to force anything. She would just go along with whatever came up now, for she was obviously incapable, she reckoned, of sorting her life out in any way.

The telephone call from Gregory came sooner than they expected. About 8 the next morning.

Jeanie sleepily went to the phone when Bill called her. 'Hi,' she said.

'Hello, baby. I'm so glad you're safe. Come home, Jeanie. All is forgiven.'

All is forgiven! Jeanie wanted to scream. What right did he think he had to be the one to be forgiving anything?

'What do you mean, forgive me? What for?' she asked, expecting him to say that it was because she had left without telling him. His reply was even more surprising:

'I know how easy it is for a woman, alone, especially in Jo'burg, to get involved with someone else. But don' worry, sweety, I understand.'

By golly! Was the man simple? The cheek of him. How dared he think I share his dirty tricks, she thought, as all sorts of retorts welled up in her throat. She swallowed hard and counted down from ten to one, while breathing deeply. Gregory waited quietly. She could almost see the smile of spite on his lips.

So, she stayed quiet. She knew that he was misinterpreting her silence for guilt, but so be it.

He arranged to fetch her later that evening. 'I'll drive you home in my car,' he said, 'then we can pick up your car tomorrow.'

'I'll drive home, thanks, Greg. I'll see you at home later.'

'Can't wait to see you later, babe.' He was happy. Anything, she knew, just to get her back into his clutches.

For the first time in years Gregory had a meal prepared for her when she arrived home. The conversation over the meal was very strained, both of them pretending to be very interested in each other's welfare.

Although not going into too much detail, she tried to explain to Gregory how she had felt and why she had left. But he did not listen. She trailed off into silence, knowing that the proper interrogation was to follow at some other time and was due to carry on for months, anyway, for he was bound not to believe a word she told him.

'Come on, Jeanie. You don't have to lie to me,' he said. 'I know you have a man in the background, and he obviously took you to Jo'burg.' It seemed to Jeanie as if he were looking for her to give him a reason for a divorce. This made her angry.

'Why do you always assume that there must be an affair in the background?'

'Why would you then suddenly up and leave me like that if it is not to go with another man?'

'I've told you a hundred times that I need to get away from you sometimes. I don't want to go into the Miranda thing...' stopping, realising that she had not spoken about Miranda to him at all before. But it was too late now. 'Is it so unnatural for a woman to do something drastic when she realises that her man is seeing someone else?'

'Don't talk to me about Miranda. That is over. Finito. Anyway, you met Miranda days before you left. If you were so heartbroken, why did you leave it so long?'

She did not know what to say, for he sounded reasonable. She sat there, miserable, mechanically stirring her tea.

'Let's try to make a fresh start, Jeanie. We have both learnt our lesson. Let's forgive and forget.'

She could not argue with that and reluctantly grunted agreement.

Making up was becoming less and less of a pleasure. In fact, it felt better for her to stay angry with him, for that way they need not pretend.

Jeanie moved back into her bedroom and, reluctantly, shared a bed with her man that night.

It was during his persistent attempts at love making to a cold, unresponsive Jeanie that night, that she realised what the lawyer had meant when he had said to her, ages ago when she had gone to see one about a divorce, 'You will know when you are ready for a divorce. And until that time arrives, nobody can push you into it.'

That time must now have arrived for she felt dead. Not a spark of desire welled up in her for the man. His passion irritated her. He nibbled at her ear, whispering lines from a love movie he had watched. How insincere he sounds, she thought, not even listening to him.

Her mind was far away while her husband pulsed inside her. She reluctantly and absentmindedly put her arms around him as his body jerked his passing into her.

All she felt was a laden, heavy coldness. An emotional void. A nothingness. She was relieved when he rolled over onto his side. She said not a word and neither did he.

With a sigh he closed his eyes and fell asleep.

Jeanie lay staring into the night, loathing herself and the man next to her. Somehow, she knew, all this would sort itself out. But when, how, and by whom, she did not know.

She was to find out much sooner than she had expected.

The next morning, after Gregory had gone to work, Jeanie had time to take stock. She sat idly at the kitchen table, lost in thought. Every day of her 32 years were showing in her face.

Elbows resting on the clean, shining kitchen table, she absentmindedly twirled her fuzzy African hair into little tressles while the chin holding up her attractive, round face, was cupped into the other palm. Her fine figure was bent forward, slumped shoulders speaking of defeat and distress.

The laughter lines around her soft brown eyes were nowhere to be seen. Her eyes were as heavy and loaded with tears as the clouds which were being driven, far beyond her empty gaze, in front of gale force winds that morning, as they constantly changed into bloated shapes and ominous forms.

A little light brown mouse ventured up to the open back door, its nostrils twitching up at her and, as her body breathed its sad fumes into the air, the mouse suddenly decided to have nothing of such melancholy and scampered back into the undergrowth in the back garden.

She saw the little mouse and also saw Gregory's favourite socks on the washing line, and it brought her vulnerability to her. Where had the love gone for the handsome man with his silky moustache?

Her marriage had brought her almost all the material things she could have wanted. She would rather have done without the comforts she had in exchange for the happiness she had thought she was wanting. The honesty and intimacy of their early days together had soon turned into half-lies and schemes.

If it was not that he has such a violent temper, she argued in his favour, we might still be quite happy together. His job as a Chartered Accountant meant that they lived very comfortably. But they were living separate lives.

For the rest of the day Jeanie hunted for a solution. She stood at the kitchen sink, looking out over Table Mountain peaking out through the two large blocks of council flats behind her house. The sky was soft and blue and she lazily stared at her neighbour's clean, fresh washing blowing in the back garden next to hers.

Jeanie thought deeply. She thought of Gregory's history of violence in his family. How many times had she heard him relate, with pride and relish, his father's 'strength' – beating up animals, 'taking no nonsense from anybody, especially his boys'. And, of course, that wives should know their place, never saying where, exactly, such a place might be.

It was not too difficult for her to see that half of Gregory's aggressiveness was not his fault. She had, though, over the years, tried to reason with him. Finally, she had stopped trying to persuade him to question his beliefs.

Challenging his attitudes had meant too much hard work, which more often than not had ended in insults being thrown at Jeanie, for he thought she was acting superior to him.

Jeanie also felt that she was, at least, not as badly off as some of the women she knew.

A friend of Mrs. Delaney's, well into her sixties, had told her gruesome stories of how she was still being knocked about by her husband after 45 years of marriage. 'I've made my bed, gotta sleep on it,' was all she could say about her powerlessness to make changes in her life.

And then there was the neighbour next door, a young woman, younger than Jeanie, whose husband beat her up regularly.

'He wakes my son up and sits him on the bed to watch me being beaten in the night,' the woman had cried. Her little boy was only two years old then.

Jeanie's heart bled for the woman, for the child, for herself and the mess they were all in, inside a culture which frowned heavily on talking to outsiders about hardships happening inside the house.

And then there was her political involvement, which Gregory had never shown any interest in. She knew that this was something about their relationship which would never change. Not now, nor after South Africa were free. Never.

And then, of course, there was Zogi.

Eventually it all became too much for her. She was too confused to know how to get out of the mess which had become her life.

Her prayers for the physical ability to strike back and hurt Gregory in the way he had done to her, of course, were never answered. In fact, violence not being a physical but a mental thing in her thinking, something which went deep into the soul, Jeanie did realise that for her to change her upbringing of non-violence so that she could attack the man physically, was out of the question. Violence and non-violence come from the inside and if not there, it is not there, she sighed.

Her only weapon was her mind. She could hand out to Gregory emotionally, the same degree of hurt which he had handed out to her. The victim Jeanie turned into the aggressor Jeanie during the next two weeks.

## Chapter 22

Gregory was humble and apologetic and seemed to genuinely be sorry for what he had done.

Jeanie was unable to forgive him. Her temporary freedom from jealousy for his affair with Miranda was short lived. Try as she might, she could not get the affair out of her mind. Promises to herself to try to be objective and adult flew out of the window as against her own better judgment and in self-destruction, she set out on a course of punishing Gregory.

Her vendetta started out simply. Such as refusing to cook, clean, do his laundry. Turning her cheek when he reached forward to kiss her. Pretending to be asleep whenever he approached her in bed.

Fuelling her mind with all his past failures, for fear that if she did not do this she would weaken. Degrading and insulting him. At every little opportunity, even to the extent of memorising, and getting into the most cutting order, the best words and phrases to use. No swearing. This would bring her down to his crawling level.

Standing in front of the mirror to perfect the facial expression of disgust like an actor rehearsing for an important performance, Jeanie listened to herself and pitched her voice for maximum effect.

Calculated, negative, soul-destroying confrontation. She carried on long conversations on the phone with people she would not normally spend time with, purposefully when Gregory was about, discussing subjects he knew nothing about, speaking in medical language and enjoying it. Going out of her way to be civil and polite to his disgusting friends who, she was aware, knew nothing about the other side of their popular, partying, happy, outgoing buddy.

'Cecil, how absolutely marvellous to see you!' she greeted his friend the next Sunday, wearing her most radiant, false smile. She could not stand the man.

On that occasion she immediately asked Gregory's friend whether he would like to enjoy some 'divine little pies which are just ready to be popped into the oven,' when she had not cooked for her man for weeks. Where he ate, she did not know, for he was always coming in late at night. She fussed around his friends. 'I know what music you are into. Listen to this. I bought it specially with you in mind.'

Gregory seethed. She ignored the signs.

And when he narrowed his eyes and turned away from her without a word, she would taunt him with 'You want to hit me, don't you! That's all you know to do properly, so why not go ahead and get it over with?' She was insolent, pushing him, taunting him, knowing of the inner fight he was having with himself.

Watching him tighten up his body in his efforts to control himself, she made sure that her derision happened when his friends were somewhere in the house, for she knew he would not touch her when they were about. With high pitched laughter she would attack him beyond closed doors as he repeatedly stormed out to vent his frustrations into beer somewhere.

The people from whom Jeanie sought advice and support were no help either. She tried to explain her predicament to some, but none of them seemed to understand. Some of them had heard of the battering handed out by Gregory. They had lots of sympathy, but no solutions, in their 'you've made your bed' culture.

And then there was Jeanie's mother, who lived out in the countryside and whom she saw very irregularly. 'I told you to leave the dog years ago,' was all her mother ever said to her. Always with wisdom and authority. Jeanie could not take her advice. Her mother never understood.

And her eldest sister who sang the gospel song, 'You can't leave him. Marriage is permanent and sacred.' She, unmarried, never even having tried to be in a relationship with a man.

Women's relief centres were only something Jeanie read about in books.

Some of her friends, especially comrades, offered some support. 'I will take you in, Jeanie, but you know how my husband is,' said her friend Judy blowing her freshly painted fingernails in comfortable suburban complacency.

'The bastard. If a man ever tries, even just lifts, his hands to me, I'll leave him immediately. And then you stand there while he has another woman!' said her 19-year-old niece, secure in her brief, uncomplicated teenage life where black is black and white is white and no grey areas exist.

'Your position presents too many legal implications, and no bank would dream of lending you money to set up on your own,' from her bank manager, making her feel like a piece of clay that had landed on his carpet.

Her lawyer was even less helpful.

She had hoped he would give her some positive ideas as to how to leave the man. She wanted to hear him tell her that she was strong enough to go through with it. She told him about their last fight and Gregory's liaison with Miranda. She wanted to hear from him that he knew she was strong enough to stand up to Gregory, to make a life on her own.

Instead, he questioned her. 'What happened last time, when you lay a charge against him for assault?' he asked as he took off his glasses and put them on his imposing mahogany desk in exasperation, while she sat on the other side, politely prepared to wait through yet another sermon.

'I withdrew the charges,' she whispered, an unnecessary answer, for he already knew it.

'You are wasting my time, Jeanie. We've been over this before. If you do not want to follow my advice, what more can I do for you?'

'But I was afraid.'

'Afraid of what?'

Afraid of the humiliation of exposing myself to smug male interviewers like you at the police station. Afraid they will say that she must have provoked Gregory. Afraid of being ignored or being told it is a domestic matter and the police do not interfere. Afraid to hear them repeat, we only took your case because your lawyer forced us. Afraid that I will lose Greg and he'd hate me for the rest of my life for leaving him to rot in jail.

All in her mind while she sat silently, wide eyed, looking at the man on the other side of the desk.

It did not dawn on Jeanie that she might look for a woman lawyer.

'...I don't know,' she said with a sigh.

With a shrug, as if explaining the impossible to an imbecile, he replied, 'Well, let's go over this again. You have a right, by law, to lay charges against him for assault if he should beat you up again.'

After the event, Jeanie thought, looking at him blankly, memories of shame flooding her mind.

'...an injunction not to come near you, which the court gave against him – when was it?' his stuffy voice forcefully pivoting her empty eyes back onto the man, '...two years ago? Still stands and you can get him imprisoned for breaking it.' He paused, waiting for her answer.

'I know that,' she said, resigned, not adding that a piece of paper signed by a registrar of a court had meant nothing at midnight in the anger and confusion of being beaten up, with a taunting 'so where is your lawyer now!' ringing in her hears.

'So, what do we do about it? You are the only one who can make up your mind about that. Nobody else can help you if you are not prepared to help yourself.' How simple it all sounded, coming from the wisdom of the law.

'I think I'm ready for a divorce now. I cannot take it any longer,' she said, making up her mind. But it did not feel quite right, she already felt, even before she said it. How does one do these things? How do you see them through?

Trying to remember dates and times, places and reasons during the next thirty minutes of note taking was painful.

'But you did not say that earlier. You are contradicting yourself again,' thrown at her with intimidating legal exactitude, time and time again, during the interview.

She left the lawyer's office on the understanding that she would contact him to let him know when he could serve the papers for divorce. And, of course, after putting down a deposit on his fees to secure his services.

'You're asking for it. I think you actually enjoy being beaten up,' said her young niece that afternoon over a cup of tea, repeating things heard in the refractory on campus, in her first year at university, knowing everything there is to know about the psychology of a battered person.

'Heard of the masochist/sadist games people play?' she rubbed it in. All Jeanie could do in response was to nod weakly.

All true through the purist eye of a psychology undergrad, eager to have found a real-life example to fit into her theory and untested methodology.

But too far removed from Jeanie's reality and feelings. True of perverts and behavioural deviants, Jeanie thought. Not true of me, defenceless woman like me. Who wants to be beaten up when all you are trying to do is to keep things together in some semblance of respectability? - her victim self-murmured from inside in self-defence.

She felt low, stupid, ugly, incapable. She joined her accusers in blaming herself for the mess which then was her life. Riddled with indecision, she added to her uncertainty and confusion by playing the negative game of vengeance.

## Chapter 23

Impulsively, on a Friday afternoon towards the end of April that year, as she often did when she needed cheering up, Jeanie decided to take a drive to Sea Point. The sea often has a soothing effect on one's thoughts, and is bound to cheer me up a bit, she reckoned.

By the time she had taken a slow walk along the esplanade and watched the sun making its spectacular departure into the sea, splashing the sky with long streaks of pink softness, she felt better. Walking back to her car she met a friend whom she had known at the hospital where she had done her training.

Jeanie immediately recognised the tall, thin, dry looking woman who walked straight towards her with a big smile on her lean face, but could not remember her name.

'I can see you can't remember me,' laughed the woman. 'It's me', Fatima. Tima, from the hospital, remember?'

'Of course, Tima! Howzit? Life treating you well?' said Jeanie, happy that she had met someone to have a chat with.

'Die lewe is grand' (Life is grand) said Tima, laughingly. Jeanie remembered the days when she used to enjoy a midnight lunch with Tima in the doctor's quarters. Tima was the night cook, then, and they had enjoyed lots of laughs together. Jeanie laughed pleasantly at the memory.

'How about coming to my place for a drink?' asked Tima. 'I've got a bottle of some fink nice there and were looking for someone nice like you to share it wif', Tima said. If Jeanie's memory was correct, Tima was Muslim and never touched alcohol. This was something new, she thought, nodding.

Together they walked around the corner to Tima's servant's room on the top floor of a 13-storey luxury apartment block. They had to squeeze in through the narrow door, which could not open properly because of the table behind it, stacked with Tima's kitchen wear. The little room was cramped with all Tima's worldly belongings. The single bed, neatly made up with a finely embroidered bed cover with matching pillowcases, stood cosily under the single window, overlooking a tidy courtyard far below.

'I did it wif my own hands,' said Tima in her best English, seeing Jeanie glance at her bed with admiration. On the little table in front of the bed, covered with a stiffly starched, white tablecloth, was a bible and radio.

'Het jy geweet ek het gedraai? (Did you know that I've converted?) Tima asked proudly, putting her hand lovingly on the bible. Jeanie smiled her surprise and Tima continued, 'Let's talk in my mother tongue, Jeanie. My English is very bad, as you know,' said in Afrikaans, and they laughed together.

Jeanie spent some time in Tima's little room, sipping away at a glass of red wine which Christianity allowed Tima to have, teasing Tima about how nice it is to be a Christian. 'That way you can now drink without worrying about who sees you.'

They were interrupted by a hasty knock on the door. Not waiting for it to be answered, the person flung the door open. It banged against the little table behind it.

'Can't you –' Tima started a reprimand, but she was interrupted by the obvious fright showing on the face of young girl who stood in the doorway.

She could not have been more than 17 years old. Her eyes big, hand half covering her mouth, she blurted out in a single breath, 'Sies (aunty) Tima, come quickly please. Thelma is screaming.'

Tima looked at Jeanie as she made for the door and Jeanie followed her into the servant's lift at the back of the building, following the frightened girl. In the lift, Tima had a chance to question the girl.

'What happened?' she asked.

'Her mother isn't here. She started screaming about half an hour ago,' said the girl, trembling slightly.

'The mother is working on the street,' Tima explained to Jeanie. 'I really want to kill the woman. She is just so stupid,' she continued.

Seeing Jeanie's puzzled expression, Tima added earnestly, her thin lips pulled together, giving emphasis to her judgment, 'If she wants to make her living selling herself, that's her thing, Jeanie. But really, when you have children –'

She trailed into silence, watching the lift indicators slowly moving down. Jeanie was even more puzzled, not knowing what to expect. Pragmatically she decided not to ask any questions until she knew what was happening.

Tima walked very fast as they came out of the lift, the young girl running ahead.

The block of flats they were heading for was two doors from Tima's building. It was a broken down, turn of the century semi-detached house. It looked as if it were standing upright with extreme difficulty, its thin pillars straining to keep up the verandah under which the women walked. Strained and cracked, its walls were covered with scales of dried out plaster, brittle and folded out, like the thickened condensations on top of a festering sore, swelling to keep the pus of degradation within.

Jeanie recognised the building as one of the many brothels which spread across this beautiful seaside town.

As they walked quickly across the back yard, a spine-chilling scream rent the air.

The room they were heading towards was on the other side of the yard, one of about ten servant's rooms. The tiny doors were closely packed next to each other.

As they neared the door in front of which their young messenger was standing, waiting for them, another high scream rose up, then sank into a deep throated gurgle, like the sound of a wounded animal.

Jeanie and Tima walked carefully past a pile of furniture stacked against the wall outside the little window before they could get to the door, which was locked. There was no curtain on the single window and two other women were bent forward outside the window, staring into the darkness beyond.

Jeanie's heart stopped at what she saw when the women stood aside for her and Tima.

The girl looked like the sounds she was making. Wild and unkempt, curly black hair stood on end in an aura of darkness around the girl's thin, pale face. Short and thin, she was standing with her back against the far wall of the little room, legs open and knees bent, both palms pressed back against the wall as if she were going to spring forward as soon as anyone moved. No more than 14 years old, it seemed, and terminally pregnant, struggling to control the uncontrollable urge to get rid of the burden in her abdomen.

As they watched, the girl let go of the wall and swung her arms around her belly. Abruptly she sat down on her haunches again, bent legs open, facing the window. Her face turned from purple to red within seconds as she pushed down like a constipated animal.

'O my God,' said Tima. 'Where is the key to the door?' as she rammed on the door handle in a panic. The young girl who had brought them to the door turned and ran back into the building to see if anyone had a key.

The girl inside was staring fixedly at them, her eyes open and frightened, glazed and fixed in an unseeing, crazy stare.

While they watched she opened her mouth wide and let out another nerve cutting scream. Her lips were too large for the v-shaped, narrow face, drawn across a hole through which projected a thick, bleeding tongue, which was trying to force itself out between sharp incisors, blood from the bruised tongue leaving a pink sediment in the corners of her mouth where it mixed with opaque, white spittle.

The long cord of a single, unlit electric bulb was swinging crazily from side to side from the ceiling. The girl must have hit it in her panic. It sneaked back and forth in the empty room as an airborne snake with a bulbous head, tail invisibly connected to the nether regions somewhere beyond the ceiling, sending mad spirits through it into the contorted figure below.

An overweight man came rushing out of the back door of the house across the courtyard. He elbowed them aside, struggling for breath through a heavy, heaving chest, unlocking the door.

The room was empty, the furniture having been stacked outside to prevent the girl from bruising herself, and the bareness gave the room an ominous, threatening mood.

Jeanie rushed over to the pregnant girl who had somehow overcome her latest contraction and was now sitting on the bare cement floor, trying to draw her bent knees nearer to her enlarged body with taught arms. Her head was bent down over her big abdomen.

She lifted her head as she heard Jeanie approach and fixed her frenzied eyes on Jeanie's face, even as her mouth opened and she let out another high pitched wail.

Nurse Dean went into action, immediately recognising the symptoms. Learning disabled, perhaps autistic, and pregnant, birth to this young girl was an experience which was as foreign as it would be to any young animal. She stared fixedly into Jeanie's face in fright. Looking into Jeanie's face all the time, again she pulled up her face and bore down, her face turning red in the effort to get rid of the baby.

'Tima,' Jeanie said, not taking her eyes off the girl's face while gently pushing the girl to get her to lie on her side, 'go and call for an ambulance and –'

'But I can't, Jeanie, I'm scared. Dunno the number. Anyway, what do I say?'

'Don't talk rubbish,' Jeanie snapped while she was trying to dislodge the girls' tight arms from her body, 'dial zero and tell the operator it's an emergency. Tell them I'm here and they must come immediately,' she panted, struggling to straighten the girls' bent legs trying to role her over onto the cold floor.

'And tell those women to fetch some blankets,' Jeanie barked as Tima rushed back outside.

'What's her name?' asked Jeanie to one of the women who had slowly come inside and was standing well away from Jeanie and the girl.

'Candy.'

'Candy,' said the nurse to the girl, who had now closed her eyes. She had gone limp under Jeanie's soft, determined touch. But the air around her reeked of anxiety and fear.

As another contraction turned her body into a massive ball on the floor, she cried out again, this time clamping her teeth into her tongue.

'Come help me,' Jeanie said quietly while she softly but firmly prized the girl's legs open, watching the girl while speaking over her back to the woman who was still standing well away from them. 'Take her arms and hold her down –', her words drowned out by another shrill cry.

Another woman came into the room and between the three of them they got the girl onto her back. While they were holding her arms firmly down by her sides on the floor, Jeanie opened her legs, indicating to them to pull up against her knees so that she could not extend them again.

'What the heck –' a man's loud voice was heard through the open window, just as Jeanie was opening the girl's vagina with her bare fingers, to see the back of a small head with wet blond hair filling the opening.

She did not look up but, from the corner of her eye, she saw highly polished black shoes under turn ups of a blue police trousers next to her as she bent over the girl on the floor.

'What's this –', he tried to say, but was shut up by a long scream as the girl bore down again.

'Go and call an ambulance, for God's sake,' Jeanie ordered, for once in her life in authority over a man: a man of the law, at that.

As he rushed out, the little pink head was born. Jeanie became oblivious to all else. She pressed the little head down gently with just enough pressure to ensure that it did not tear the girl's tight virginal passage.

With a heave and without instruction, the girl pushed down again, this time ejecting the whole of the little infant in one smooth movement, birth fluid rushing out onto the cement floor, soaking into Jeanie's ankle length dress, where it was caught under her knees.

Jeanie had just enough time to cup her hands and catch the tiny, smooth body as it slid out from between its mother's outer vagina with the smoothness and agility of a slippery eel.

The baby cried loudly, even before the nurse had a chance to take the edge of her long skirt to wipe the wee face. Premature and wrinkled, she looked like a dry old lady at the end of life.

Jeanie had not looked up once since she walked through the door. A blanket was handed down to Jeanie, and she placed the baby on it, carefully covering it from the cold and harshness of the world it had entered.

Their eyes had been on the baby and suddenly Candy twisted herself upright, back against the wall, with the umbilical cord still attached to the baby and the placenta inside her. Fortunately, Jeanie had the baby quite close to Candy who bent forward and tried to grab the baby from Jeanie's hands. Jeanie firmly pushed her extended arms against her chest with one hand and forced her to lie back while she held the baby at a safe distance.

The girl made a threatening, gurgling sound deep inside her throat as she stared straight into Jeanie's eyes. But she was too weak to resist and flopped tiredly back onto the cement floor, closing her eyes and collapsed as if her life had drained out of her with the baby.

This gave Jeanie a chance to press lightly on the near unconscious girl's abdomen to feel for a further contraction, which is vital for delivery of the placenta. She heard the siren of the ambulance which went quiet within seconds as it stopped in the street. Even as she heard the ambulance staff run across the courtyard, a contraction came, and Candy instinctively and easily, in her half-conscious state, pushed the afterbirth out.

Jeanie had a quick look at the placenta, which was red and healthy, as the ambulance paramedics rushed through the door and placed a stretcher on the floor next to the girl. The ambulance assistant quietly came closer, and

Jeanie was able to move aside. She had a spasm in her right calf and her back ached as she stood up.

She did not wait to see the placenta being separated from the baby, and tiredly walked past the small crowd of people who had by now cramped into the courtyard outside the now closed door. She went to the outside tap against the wall and let the gushing, cold, clean water wash away the stains of blood and secrets of the mentally disordered mind which she had left behind in a cold, sad, empty room.

As she walked back across the yard, she met Tima.

Wordlessly the two women walked back the way they had come, their long-delayed friendship further delayed.

# Chapter 24

Jeanie decided to leave. Tima was a bit disappointed as 'It is rude to leave before the bottle is empty,' she said to Jeanie. But Jeanie was feeling slightly depressed about her experience and the afternoon.

Also, she had come to a decision.

She stood up and was reaching for her bag, when they heard a voice through the half-closed door. 'Sies Tima, you there? What happened with Candy?', followed by a light knock on the door.

Jeanie had heard that low, sexy voice somewhere before. She frowned in an effort to remember where she had heard it, when the woman opened the door.

They both went rigid with shock.

They faced each other, neither one able to say a word, while Tima looked from one to the other, wondering what was happening. Realising something was wrong, Tima tried weakly to give an introduction. 'Jeanie, this is – ', but abruptly changed her mind as she saw the faces of the two women recognising each other. 'You – you know each other?' she stammered in rough Afrikaans, surprised.

Neither woman answered nor looked at her. In fact, neither of them had even heard her, it seemed.

Jeanie was too shocked at what she saw to know what to do next. She almost fell down back onto Tima's bed from which she had just stood up.

It was Miranda who regained her composure first.

She carefully closed the door and stood with her back leaning against it. One of her slim, long legs, which had caused Jeanie so many hours of envy, was casually folded over the other, the light brown, soft milky skin of her upper thigh a stark contrast to the knee-high velvet lace-up boots which she was wearing.

Jeanie's eyes slowly rose up the long legs, wondering when they would end, up over a very tiny leather shorts, creased in the groin in its attempt to hold onto Miranda's thin abdomen. An attractive belly button nuzzled in the middle of a smooth, bare mid-rift. Jeanie's eyes wondered up to a skimpy and, of course, black, silk brassiere, inadequately trying to cover light brown nipples which were peeping out over the black laces which strained to contain half-exposed breasts.

She could not believe what she was seeing.

The little room was quiet.

Tima was holding her breath, covering her mouth with her hand, instinctively knowing that something was going to blow up, not knowing what.

Miranda gave one of her red-mouthed, wide smiles and said quietly, 'Surprised?' almost teasing poor Jeanie.

'What you see is true, my rival. I'm a prostitute. Full time.'

Jeanie looked to Tima in embarrassment, and Tima gave a small nod.

'Make some tea for the lady, Sies Tima,' Miranda continued, a pleasant gurgle starting up in her throat, her eyes softening in amusement at Jeanie's discomfort and disbelief. 'She needs it desperately.'

Tima squeezed between the two women to get to the table behind the door next to Miranda, to start the electric kettle. Jeanie watched her bend down to insert the plug into the socket under the table, procrastinating the moment of truth, as Tima filled up the kettle from a jug of water which was standing on the little table.

The kettle had started to boil by the time Jeanie regained her composure. She turned her eyes to Miranda and lost her nerve when she met the relaxed amusement on the woman's face. She looked fixedly at Miranda, all her good training and manners forgotten.

Miranda in the meantime, having seen the half bottle of wine at the bedside, casually took two of her long strides, reached out for one of the glasses, and poured a glass full of wine, which she handed to Jeanie.

'If you wanna fight, sister, that's fine by me. But this time, I'll win,' she said with a giggle, the soft look in her eyes belying her words as she looked Jeanie straight in the eyes. As she said it, she stood with the glass of wine in her outstretched hand, waiting for Jeanie to decide whether to accept it.

It took Jeanie a while to make up her mind. Eventually, with a shrug she reached out and took the glass from Miranda's hand. She did not drink from it, but held it between her hands, her palms cupped around the top of the glass, as if she were seeking strength from the red liquid inside it. Miranda took the other glass, filled it up to the brim, threw her head back and gulped half of it down as if it were a glass of water.

'How do you know each other?' asked Tima in a timid voice. She looked a bit excited now, eagerly turning around to look at each of the women in turn, while Jeanie and Miranda stared at each other like two cats about to grab at each other.

Then, in a relaxed movement, Miranda sat down on the bed and patted the space next to her for Jeanie to join her.

'Come now, girls. No fighting in your aunt's house,' said Tima in relief, looking at Jeanie, then at Miranda, who smiled her encouragement. 'For heaven's sake, Jeanie, sit down and act like a woman!'

Jeanie took the seat and, as soon as she sat down, Miranda put her arm around Jeanie's shoulders and gave them a squeeze. This relaxed Jeanie.

'We met -,' she started.

'I've been whoring with her husband,' Miranda coarsely said to the room, her eyes on Jeanie, pleased to see the blood rush to Jeanie's cheeks.

Jeanie nodded wearily.

Tima was immediately inquisitive. 'How did you find out, Jeanie?' not able to keep a smile from her face. 'Did you catch this cow on the job with your man?' Her eyes met Miranda's and both of them burst out in laughter.

Jeanie felt a confusion of emotions which she could not understand. She looked at the women enjoying her discomfort. She at first held her head down, scowling at the wine. Then she looked up at the two of them with a frown, meaning to shut them up with her seriousness.

But this made them laugh louder. They could not stop. In her amusement, Miranda brought her knees up to her chin while at the same time swinging her arm in an exaggerated half circle, hit herself on the forehead, and threw her head back, her eyes brimming over with tears.

Tima was by this time holding her stomach with one hand, trying to shut out the sound of her laughter with the other by closing her mouth, not wanting to hurt Jeanie.

But they could not stop laughing and this affected Jeanie. Her quick mind took a long time to grasp the ridiculousness of her situation. A slow smile spread across her face and, seeing this, the other two laughed all the more. By this time Jeanie was unable to keep a straight face. Whether out of relief that the mood of the moment had changed or for whatever reason, she started laughing with them. Seeing this, the other two screamed in merriment, and Jeanie let go completely.

Within a minute Jeanie was well into it and her cheek muscles started aching in their effort to pull her face back into seriousness. Her infectious gurgle speeded up as it changed into a higher octave and the three women went into uncontrolled laughter.

'How -,' Tima still wanted her curiosity satisfied.

'None of your bleeding business!' said Miranda, and the three of them went into fresh fits of laughter.

Slowly they settled down. Miranda pulled a bright red silk handkerchief from the back of her little shorts and wiped her eyes. Jeanie reached for the bottom of her long, wide skirt, but stopped herself just in time when she felt how wet it still was, and wiped her eyes with her sleeve, while Tima pulled her hand across her face, the last bit of a smile closing over her big teeth.

## Chapter 25

They sat in silence for a minute while Tima handed around the tray which she had prepared, dainty cups matching a beautiful teapot.

'I'd better serve you, Jeanie,' said Miranda jokingly, jumping up and pouring Jeanie's tea. 'Milk, sugar, madam?'

This started them off again and they carried on laughing while sipping the lovely tea, like old friends.

Miranda, in honest openness, in a low voice, then started telling Jeanie how she had met Gregory. It was at one of their business cocktails. She had accompanied one of her clients that night, Miranda said. Jeanie, marvelling at Miranda's honesty, said nothing, awed by the woman's ease and friendliness.

Respect was starting to grow between the two women who lived in such different worlds.

Jeanie had not said much and Miranda, sensitively, now no longer smiling, said to her, 'Ask me anything you like, Jeanie. I have no secrets that I'm not prepared to share.'

Jeanie felt relieved, but did not ask any questions, not wanting to know too much about the relationship which might by now be over. She sat quietly there with her doubts, unsure what to do next.

It was once again Miranda who intuitively came to her rescue. 'Ok, Jeanie. I know how you feel, and I respect you for your reserve. I'm sorry if I caused you pain. It was not until I saw you at the car that day that I knew how hard it must be for you.'

Jeanie looked at Miranda in gratitude. What a sensitive person this was!

This gave her the courage to say to Miranda, 'Don't feel sorry for me, Miranda. I think I knew that my marriage was over long before you came along. But –'

She stopped, expecting an interruption. But as none came, she continued, 'I've been wasting so much of my energy on jealousy –'

'And all unnecessary, hey?' interrupted Miranda to reassure her. Jeanie dropped her eyes and went quiet.

'Jeanie,' said Miranda softly. They had forgotten Tima, who was sitting in the little chair next to the table behind the door, listening.

'Jeanie, you are married to a very bad man, you know that, don't you.'

Jeanie looked up at Miranda in agreement. 'Yes, he's a wife beater. Did you know that, too, Miranda?'

'I know more than that, Jeanie. I'm sorry to have to tell you this, but I think you should know.'

Jeanie held her breath, knowing something devastating was on its way. She stared at Miranda with resignation, with a strong intuition.

'I don't think Tima knows this,' Miranda turned to look at Tima, who said nothing. 'Your bastard of a husband has been sexually abusing the young daughter of one of the girls.'

'What? Really? How old is the child?'

'It's been carrying on for about a year now. The child is no more than 11 years old. I know because the girl has told her mum, who is afraid to report it to the police.'

'Why?'

'Because, my dear, we are women of the street, and the cops don't care about us or what happens to our children. Do you think they would believe this family against your upright husband in his shiny Chartered Account suit?'

Jeanie could just nod. Her disgust was beyond words.
'Don't even think of asking him about it, Jeanie. He will just deny it and then you will be in very big trouble. Trust me, I do know what men are like. And your Gregory is not a real man!'

At that moment Jeanie decided that her little game with the diamond pendant was over. She said to Miranda, 'I have your necklace. If you want to arrange for us to meet sometime, let me know.'

It was Miranda's turn to look surprised. Open eyed in amazement and admiration, she said, 'You're a very clever woman, Jeanie. Yes, I'd like to meet you again.'

That night, lying in the little bed in their spare room, Jeanie listened to Gregory snoring next door. Strangely, she was not very angry. She felt more than anger. She felt deep, deeply sorry. Sorrow for the three of them who had become caught up in the trap of adult confusion. Sorry for Gregory. Disgust for him so deep that she could not even cry.

The moment which her lawyer had waited for had arrived. She was going to leave him, no matter how violent or threatening he was. She was going to leave him, with or without possessions. Her life and dignity were more important to her than his money and security.

## Chapter 26

Tiredly she fell asleep that night and woke up very early next morning, well before Gregory came out of the main bedroom. She had decided to speak to him when he got back home later, but do her nursing rounds first.

Her calmness surprised her. She had thought that the worst part about parting would be the decision to do so. But, in the end, the decision was the easier part of the whole affair.

She did not know how she suddenly came to know, as surely as she was confident that things would work out for her somehow, that she was moving out. How, when, where to, she still did not know. And, wisely, she did not plan this in detail, deciding to let things happen. She would merely tell Gregory this afternoon that she was leaving and would make her arrangements sometime over the weekend.

Her first call that Saturday morning was to the house of a young mother whose baby Nurse Douglas had delivered the Wednesday before.

Jeanie knew that the woman's boyfriend was not at home and, as was usual, she gave a single knock on the front door and opened the little bedsit in Bishop Lavis. As she walked into the little room with its smell of depressing poverty and struggle, she went through one of those contradictions again, which faced her so often.

Bishop Lavis, also known as kill me quick town, was one of the most dangerous areas in Cape Town. Yet the young woman was lying there on her little bed with an open door, her other two toddlers playing on the threadbare little carpet in front of her.

Jeanie was about to reprimand her, inviting trouble by leaving the door unlocked on a Saturday morning with doped up and drunk men walking past her window only a few metres from where she lay. But there was no sense in doing this. It would just be imposing her own insecurities onto the poor woman, who looked quite relaxed and happy, sitting up in her little bed, cuddling and singing to her newborn while keeping a watchful eye over her other two children.

'Hello, nurse,' the woman's eyes lit up when she saw Jeanie. 'Sorry about the mess.' She apologised unnecessarily, looking up at Jeanie, from whom she got the hoped for, sympathetic and understanding smile. Satisfied, she moved carefully further back onto the bed after laying the baby down on the bed at her feet.

One look at the baby told the nurse that it had become quite jaundiced. She looked the woman and carefully picked the baby up. The woman had suspected nothing.

Jeanie walked over to the little window with the baby while saying to the mother 'Hi Agatha. Did you sleep well?' while she held the infant up to the natural light to look at its colour properly. She turned to the mother, who was watching her intently. 'It looks like your little one is a bit more yellow today,' she said.

'Really?' said Agatha, concerned. 'I didn't see it.'

'That's because you have not been out of your house, Agatha. Come to the sunlight.'

Agatha slowly swung her legs off the low bed and took a few steps over to where Jeanie was standing with the baby. Typically postnatal, her back was arched, and she kept her hand on her delicate abdomen. She walked with slow steps, trying to keep her legs together so as not to stretch the absorbable stitches still keeping her outer vaginal wall together, where the birth had torn her passage.

Jeanie smiled slightly, looking at her, enjoying the familiar gentleness and warmth of after birth. Conscious of her body and its miraculous powers, Agatha was caring and nurturing it. Agatha, who was a very heavy smoker and drinker, had lost her desire for these habits completely during the last few months. And Jeanie, looking at her conscientious protection of her body, hid her wonderment under the soft smile on her face.

'O yes,' said Agatha, putting her finger over the soft little face as if to feel the change in colour. 'You are right. What does that mean, nurse?'

'It happens often,' said the nurse. 'Especially before they are three days old. Their little livers have to adjust to the new eating habits and this might show that her liver is not quite used to the change.'

'Oh,' replied Agatha, none the wiser, a puzzled look on her face.

'I don't think it is anything serious, Agatha, but the jaundice does look a bit heavy this morning. I think that it might be best if we had her watched in hospital for a day or so.'

Agatha's face dropped. 'Can't we keep her here? I'll watch her ever so carefully,' she ventured, but stopped when the nurse shook her head.

'I'll feel much better if she is under constant care at the hospital, Agatha. Rather lose a day without her than to be unsure,' said the nurse.

With slow, painful movements Agatha walked back to the bed, turning to position the back of her knees against the bedstead and reaching backwards with outstretched arms for support, before lowering her body onto the bed slowly.

Jeanie walked over to her and helped her back into bed after she had lain the baby down. Agatha nodded wordlessly as the nurse said to her, 'That will give you a chance to rest, too. You look wiped out.'

While Jeanie was lighting the primus stove which stood on a table in an alcove under the window facing the backyard of the block of flats, she reassured Agatha. Soon the two women were chatting away, while Jeanie waited for the water which she had put on the stove to heat up, so that she could give the baby its bath.

'Have you had a wash today, Agatha?' she asked. 'If not, I might as well give you one, and the whole family,' Jeanie said laughingly, pointing towards the little brother and sister obediently and in childlike oblivion, playing with an old ball on the floor.

'O yes, we've all had our wash,' said Agatha, happily, going on to explain 'Derek is so good. He gave them a bath last night when he came home and did me before he went to work at five this morning.' She said this with satisfaction, waiting for the compliment.

'You're a very lucky devil, you know,' the nurse said on cue. Agatha needed this, for her life offered her not much fun or enjoyment.

This opened Agatha up and, while Nurse Dean was swabbing her tender vaginal area down and clearing a part of the bed to put the baby on after its bath, she happily talked about her plans of a more abundant life, brightening up the little room with her dreams.

Jeanie took much longer than she should have done with Agatha that morning. It was a pleasure for her to make some porridge in one of the only two pots in the kitchen area after she had bathed the baby.

Then, sitting down on the bed next to her satisfied patient, she watched her and her children fill themselves up with the mealiepap, the little room once again tidy, which she had done, guided by Agatha.

'Nurse Dean,' said Agatha before Jeanie left. 'I really would like for one of my children to become a nurse one day. I will never forget you.'

'Bless you, and thank you, Agatha,' she replied, humbly. She did not know what else to say as she stood with her case in her hand, ready to leave. 'I will ask the doctor to send an ambulance for the baby to be taken to hospital later.'

But Agatha continued, her eyes bright with admiration, 'I know that what you do for us you do not have to do as part of your work, nurse. All the women I speak with in the area think you are great. I wish there was more we could give you.'

Jeanie did not know exactly how much her patients would need to do for her soon.

## Chapter 27

Early evening on that Saturday, which completely changed Jeanie's life, she arrived home to find Gregory's car in the driveway.

She started thinking of her own situation only as she parked the car, her work having, as always, given her the chance to forget about her own problems, for which she was always very grateful.

Gregory was in the sitting room, half the bottle of Vodka which had been in the liquor cabinet in his body, the other half on the coffee table in front of him. Seeing this, Jeanie decided not to rock the boat.

Ignoring him, she walked straight past him to the bedroom, put her midwifery bag down and changed into a long floral skirt and light cardigan. She was just about to walk to the back door, thinking it best to get out of his way for a while, when he shouted from the sitting room, 'Jeanie, I want to talk with you!' She walked back and stood in the doorway.

Her heart started to beat faster.

'What time did you get in last night?'

'Before nine.'

'Where were you?'

'Working.'

'Don't lie to me!'

'I'm not lying.' Her body was by now trembling.

'Jeanie, don't look for trouble. Just answer my question,' threateningly.

'I told you. I was working.'

'I tell you, woman, if I should find out that you're seeing another man, I'll kill both of you!' His suspicions and threats were getting too much. She stared at him, trying to decide how to respond.

Then her fear left her completely. Putting her arms in her sides, she said, 'You're the one who's messing around, not me. Don't try to project your guilt onto me.'

'You're being cheeky. Don't push me too far!' He was by now shouting.

Keeping her voice down, she said quietly, 'I met your Miranda yesterday.'

'My who –' For a moment he did not connect the name, it seemed. Then the muscles in his face became hard, concrete and white. 'How dare you go snooping around, prying into my business!'

'Do you call finding out that you're still seeing the woman snooping around?' Before he had a chance to reply, she continued, now hardly aware of what she was saying, 'And I knew, too, that you have been exploiting the woman.' Strange that I can't call Miranda a prostitute to this man, she thought, wondering why she was protecting Miranda.

'What do you know about any of this?' His silly question showed his surprise.

'I know that you have been telling her bullshit about a divorce. I know that you are a –.' Just in time she stopped herself from calling him a paedophile. But the thought made her too angry for reason. 'You're a spineless bastard you know that?'

A backhanded slap across her face stopped her. She fell with a thump against the wall behind her and steadied herself. When she came up, she saw Gregory locking the front door, pocketing the key as he came back to her.

'You're not going to hit me this time,' she screamed, fear making her limbs go weak.

'I'll teach you a lesson once and for all. I'll show you,' he shouted as he grabbed her thick hair and dragged her to the front door. Her body was limp and heavy, and he struggled to get her to the wall next to the door, where he knocked her head repeatedly against the wall.

She must have fainted, because when she next came to, she was on the floor, blood streaming down in her face, Gregory's heavy feet kicking her in the ribs while she lay cowering. She flung her arms out in a weak attempt to get to her feet.

He had lost control completely.

She opened her mouth to scream, but this time just a little squeak came out. Horrified, she saw him lift his right foot and stamp it down hard on her right hand.

The pain was so intense that it seemed to give her the strength to get onto her knees. She had to get away from the raving lunatic.

For some reason Gregory had turned around, away from her. This gave her a chance to push herself onto her knees and she crawled into the passage and through the small kitchen, to the open back door. She came upright as she reached the door and, with superhuman strength, ran around the house without a sound, past the still closed front door and out through the gate.

The blood was blinding her, but she kept running, her feet carrying her along with a will of their own.

## Chapter 28

Jeanie had not had much sleep since Saturday.

She had tried to dose off on hard benches in the waiting room at hospital in the emergency room, where she had spent all Saturday night, then the police station Sunday and Sunday night, afraid to go home.

She felt dizzy with hunger and fright, as she had all weekend, scared that Gregory might turn up and find her, even in the police waiting room. She was terrified of Gregory's power. She had cringed every time the charge office door had opened expecting Gregory to walk through the door.

Jeanie had no idea of how the wheels of legal procedures turn. She did not know that once the charge of Assault and Grievous Bodily Harm had been written down, a policeman had gone to arrest Gregory. Neither did she know that he had spent the night in the same police station for the last 24 hours!

She wondered what would happen next, dazed, feeling and looking dirty and dishevelled, as she wondered about aimlessly in the street that Monday morning.

She walked past the street where they lived, along the busy thoroughfare, jumping out of the way of hooting sixteen seater combies which served as cheap transport for people going to work. The workers' taxis, two people sitting next to each other on one seat, nudging each other and pushing to find comfort while the taxi rocked recklessly as it overtook cars and mounted pavements to get to nowhere first.

Jeanie jumped out of the way on the edge of the road which served as a dust-edged pavement. She had no money on her, so could not get onto a bus or taxi.

In her confusion she just thought about her job. She needed to retrieve the car, to go and find out what was happening at work.

She did not know that Gregory had been taken to the courthouse, charged and let out on bail until the hearing.

Much later, having walked up the Klipfontein Road, two kilometres to Athlone, tired and distressed, Jeanie knocked on Ellen's white painted door.

Explaining to her friend and Charles, Ellen's husband what had happened took hours. It was late before Jeanie finally settled on the little bed in Ellen's back yard, in the out-room known as the servant's room.

## Chapter 29

Jeanie woke up in a sweat and cried out loud when she realised where she was at three the next morning.

The dream was very vivid. Mixed with half-truths twisted into different shapes with heaving emotions, she saw Jeanie, as she had seen her in real life that fateful night last year.

Then Gregory had still been the only man who knew how to find Jeanie's deepest liquid self. She dreamt how she had trembled, trying to push herself up to him deep inside her. Her eyes level with his hairy chest, she wondered, fleetingly, where his firm stomach muscles were going. Might they still be there somewhere, hidden under the fat which shuddered under her arms as he came down into her?

Suddenly he rolled over, out of her, just as a wave of completion rose up, stopping it. Before she knew what had happened, he was up, out of bed, reaching for his dressing gown, rushing through the door.

In the dream her anger was instant, all-consuming. It boiled over her throbbing insides, flushing hot blood over her cheeks. Tears welled up, forcing her to close her eyes. Her rebuffed body went rigid as two hot tears cursed down the sides of her upturned face into her ears.

Through her distress and anger, she heard voices, his voice and another's, on the other side of the then closed bedroom door in her dream.

Jeanie saw herself lay suspended in a pool of rejection. Slowly the fear, which she had been suppressing all that evening, clawed its darkness back into her mind, shadowing even her anger.

He was, after all, her ex-husband, she dreamt through a scramble of time and space. She had told herself that all of that evening, when she had known that they'd end up in bed together after all those years of fighting and hatred.

They had talked about their old irritations which, after seven years, had lost their intensity in some parts, as old curtains lose their colour in places exposed to the sun of experience and hardship. They had laughed about the insipidness of their silly jealousies, and they had become friends again. Or so she'd thought. In her dream it felt good and real.

Between kisses and foreplay, the second half of the bottle of Chardonnay had disappeared into both of them unnoticed, and suddenly the bottle had been empty. This she remembered. She also remembered running eagerly past her clothes and shoes, leaving them in a pile on the floor in the sitting room. Naked evidence still lying there.

But that did not matter. What did matter was that she had just given herself to a man whom she had vowed never to allow into her inner emotions, or self, ever again. She had failed herself. She had allowed him to reach her.
Without a condom.

'We've known each other a long time,' she remembered him whispering in her ear, 'we go back a long way, Jeanie,' he'd side-stepped her request that they use a condom, and she had nodded agreement as she sipped the wine.

And after all that, he'd just jumped up, out of her, his body still glistening with – what she had been sure of, was still sure of – his need of her. He had rejected her.

A wave of hatred swept away the fear.

Suddenly the bedroom door flew open. Jeanie lay rigid. A woman's voice came in ahead of a big body, which Jeanie could see in the full-length mirror on the other side of the bed.

Then the woman came around the wardrobe and saw her. Jeanie was shocked. She did not try to sit up in bed, just pulled the covers closer around her naked body.

The woman stared into Jeanie's face, but did not seem to notice her. Jeanie realised with amazement that the woman was so comfortable with her surroundings and confident within herself, that another woman, naked in bed in front of her, was just a small matter. An irrelevance, which could be sorted out later, not important right then.

The woman put an overnight bag on the chest of drawers facing the bed, and for an instant turned her well-corseted fourteen stone buttocks to Jeanie inside a tailored burgundy suit. Then she turned back to face Jeanie, white teeth showing between perfect lips, painted a very dark colour, a shade darker than her almost navy velvet skin. Her recently permed hair flamed out in an attractive black cloud above smooth skin stretched tightly over high cheekbones.

'You can take the spare room,' she said to Jeanie with a slight smile, not the least bit perturbed, not curious.

Jeanie jumped up, folding the bedcovers around her small forsaken frame, and fled from the bedroom. She came level with the women's close-set sparkling black eyes as she pushed herself past the other's bulk through the door.

The woman's naturally smiling lips curled up into a full-blown smile as she stared past Jeanie at the figure of their mutual man, now standing facing the bedroom in knee-length shorts twisted in a hurried angle of panic around a bulky middle.

It was three in the morning.

Jeanie's purse was still lying on the couch where she had dropped it an hour earlier, before her short-lived surrender into evasive ecstasy. The alcohol, typical coward that it was, had fled, taking its pleasant fuzziness with it, leaving her head throbbing, her mouth dry. She felt cold, her body having left its heat behind in the bedroom, to warm up the intimate murmur behind the once again closed door.

Her rejection was complete. She sat down on the couch, inside the big duvet, pulled her feet up under her, too tired and confused to know what to do.

After a few minutes he appeared. She could still taste the bile when she woke up out of the nightmare. It rushed into her throat and her head had screamed at her. She swallowed hard, as, in semi-consciousness, trying to come out of the nightmare, she tried to clear her head in confusion, immediately slipping again into her dream world.

'Sorry,' he began, throwing out his arms, and the sight of the pathetic, trembling flab of the middle-aged failure of her one-time man swept like a panacea over her nausea.

She felt sorry for him, sorry for herself, for her foolishness. In fact, more fed up with her stupidity than with his carelessness.

Wearily Jeanie threw on her dress, stuffing her knickers and bra into her bag.

'I did not expect her,' she heard him mumble from under an overgrown moustache as the front door slammed behind her tired back.

She stopped to put on her shoes only when she had turned the corner into the high street to hail a taxi.

As she got into the cab, she realised that she'd left her purse behind.

That woke her up in a sweat. She sat bolt upright, remembering, confused, in a surreal world of darkness in Ellen and Charles' back yard room.

It was late that Monday morning that she eventually remembered that she had been given a medical certificate by the doctors at the hospital the day before, declaring her unfit for work until her ribs, hand and wound in her head had healed.

# Chapter 30

The state prosecutor searched through a brown folder.

'The State versus Gregory Dean, Case No 13021 of 1975' he said, as he handed some papers to the magistrate, who was sitting behind his high desk looking anaemic and sombre. The prosecutor promptly sat down.

'Will the accused please stand', said the Magistrate.

'I represent the accused, your Worship,' a lawyer jumped up, pulling his black gown forward over a big belly.

Jeanie went into a panic. So, he had a lawyer!

The lawyer sat down. It was the prosecutor's turn to jump up. The rapid standing up and sitting down would have been funny to her had she not been in such a state herself.

'The charge, in terms of Section 171 of the Criminal Procedure Act, is that Gregory Dean did on Saturday, the 7th day of August 1975, cause grievous bodily harm to one Jennifer Dean,' he recited from the file in his hand.

Jeanie did not look at Gregory. She had caught him from the side of her eye as he was brought up from the staircase leading directly from the cells under the courthouse into the front of the court room. She was sitting at the back, and he had not seen her from where he was sitting next to his attorney facing the front.

She could see his upper lip twitch as he bit on his lower jaw, the muscles in his right cheek, which she saw from an angle, jumping. She was obviously not the only person who was nervous. She had not seen him since that night, more than a month ago and she felt slightly pleased by his concentrated, unshaven look.

'Will the accused please stand,' from the Magistrate. Gregory stood up in humble sobriety.

'How do you plead?'

'Not guilty.'

'Mr…' frowned the magistrate, trying to remember the lawyer's name.

'Kolowski,' the lawyer jumped up and sat down immediately, swinging his heels and pulling up his trousers importantly while rubbing his chin knowingly. His actions intimidated Jeanie to whom it seemed that he was making it clear that his client was about to walk free any moment. She cringed and felt awfully alone in the alien building with its high ceilings and imposing, big, oak-lined walls.

'Is your client making any admissions, Mr Kolowski?' Jumping up, 'No sir,' sitting down.

The prosecutor seemed more agile than a twelve-year-old at first communion. In his practiced rush not to be outdone by Kolowski's calisthenics, he almost knocked over the bottle of water standing on his desk. 'I call the State's sole witness, Jennifer Dean.'

Jeanie did not hear this. She sat almost hypnotized by the agility of the impressive executors of the law. She woke up, as if out of a dream, hearing the Court Bailiff shout into the passage, 'Jennifer Dean! Jennifer Dean!'

In her confusion to scramble up and grab her handbag at the same time, adjusting her long skirt which suddenly got entangled with the sharp edge of the seat, she almost ran forward, and tripped on the step leading to the front platform in front of the huge bench where the clerk of the court and stenographer sat in front of the magistrate's high chair.

Embarrassed, feeling like a fool, she was shown into the witness box. She caught a glimpse of the policeman who had taken her statement, almost midday that Sunday, after she had been sitting in the smelly police charge office since the previous Saturday afternoon. He gave her no encouragement. In fact, he did not even seem to recognise her. Jeanie felt lost in a world of dominant, unsympathetic, uncompromising, men.

Another man in a black robe, his face pale and drawn, lifted a shaking hand, DTs, Jeanie thought, looking at his sagging mouth and red nose as he faced her. 'What is your name?' he asked.

'Jennifer -,' her voice squeaked, and she cleared her throat. 'Jennifer Dean.' 'Will you please speak clearly and address the Bench?' he said sternly.

She turned her head to the magistrate, repeating her name in a quiet gurgle through a blob of mucous in the back of her throat.

'Do you swear to tell the truth, the whole truth and nothing but the truth? Raise your right hand and say so help me God.' Jeanie mutely obeyed.

The prosecutor sounded bored and irritable as he addressed her. 'Tell the Court what happened on Saturday, 7th August.'

That was three months ago. Where could she start?

Everyone was looking at her. The entire court room was quiet. Should I start with Miranda? Or should I talk about the argument on Saturday morning? She looked lost and bewildered.

'Did you hear the question, Mrs. Dean? I will repeat it. Will you tell the Court what happened on Saturday, 7th August this year? Please speak into the microphone to the Bench, not to me,' for Jeanie had again shifted her face away from the magistrate.

'We were arguing, and he had been drinking early the morning.'

'What was he drinking?'

'Vodka.'

Kolowski jumped up and on his side of the sea saw, the prosecutor sat down. 'That is irrelevant, your Worship.'

'What's irrelevant, Mr. Kolowski – that your client had been drinking or that he is alleged to have been drinking vodka?' asked the magistrate.

'That he had been drinking, Sir.'

The rest of the discourse was lost on Jeanie. Her mind was running like a computer screen trying to find the beginning of her story. Was it better to skip all the horrid things she knew from what Miranda had told her, or should she get right into the nightmare itself? How much time are they giving me to talk? Am I allowed to say it like it happened or do they expect legal language from me? She stared at the magistrate, big brown eyes glazed over in fright and confusion, blinking away the silly tears which were blinding her.

'Carry on, Mrs. Dean,' the magistrate said, and Jeanie felt she was in purgatory as she wet her lips, watching the lawyer and prosecutor pop down, two white bald patches shining in the fluorescent court lights.

'I can't remember exactly how it happened because it was so quick,' she said. 'I remember that he locked the front door so that I could not run out of the house. He put the key into his pocket. He grabbed me and hit my head against the wall next to the front door, where he had dragged me. He kept banging my head against the wall. The blood was running down my face and neck.' She spoke fast now, the words rushing out of her mouth as the whole horrific scene opened itself up in her frightened mind.

'He did not stop banging my head against the wall. When I became too weak to stand up, I fell down on the floor. Then he kicked me and stamped on my hand.' It all poured out. Reliving this caused her extreme distress and in her consternation, she felt the pain in her lung, where the broken rib was pressing against her chest. She could hardly breathe, and her hand was still aching, despite the fact that the splint with which they had secured it, had been removed. She gasped and rubbed her hand gently, getting some comfort from the gentle feel of her warmth against the coldness of her surroundings.

She knew that she was expected to say more but, incredibly, there was no more to be said. All her unhappiness, hurt, discomfort had been fit into a few sentences in less than two minutes. She bent her head so that Gregory would not see the tears scorching down her hot cheeks.

'Did you sustain any bruises?' the magistrate asked. What a silly question, Jeanie thought, and the prosecutor saved her from answering.

'Yes Sir,' he said, again on his feet. 'I have a doctor's report here, showing that Mrs. Dean had to receive six stitches to her scalp from a two-inch laceration, and had two metacarpals broken in her right hand, plus two ribs on her right side.' He handed the report to the clerk who took it to the bench.

Jeanie involuntarily put her hand on her head for it had started to ache where the hair had started growing over the then shaven patch. The magistrate noticed this.

'Are you feeling unwell, Mrs. Dean?' he asked her.

Jeanie dropped her arm awkwardly and felt embarrassed as all eyes were again turned to her. She said nothing.

'Will the Clerk of the Court please inspect the wound on Mrs. Dean's head,' the magistrate actually said, and Jeanie went into a real panic. A sideways glance at Gregory told her that he was getting a lot of satisfaction out of her awkwardness, for he had a faint smile on his face.

By this time the old clerk was climbing up the three steps into the witness box and stood next to her. Jeanie was hot with embarrassment.

Sheepishly she turned to look up at the old man. His eyes were kindly and he smiled down at her, waiting for her to turn her head so he could look at the wound.

He put his hand on her arm, bent down to her ear, and softly whispered 'come now, lassie, don't be afraid. It will be alright,' the first kind words she had heard in these alien surroundings.

A strong smell of beer floated into her face as he smiled into her face. It gave her the strength temporarily to forget herself as she bent her head so he could look down on the wound. The kindly man, instinctively appreciating the trauma of Jeanie's experience, kept his hand on her arm, giving it a slight pressure of encouragement.

'I see a wound under the short hair which has grown over it. It is about three inches long,' he said, at the same time handing Jeanie a soft, white tissue to dry her eyes. The wound was throbbing.

'Would you like rest, Mrs. Dean?' the magistrate asked kindly.

'No thank you, Sir. I feel ok' she stood up and whispered, her neck stiff, avoiding turning to the audience. The magistrate nodded and wrote something down.

'Is that all, Mr. Prosecutor?' he asked when he looked up.

'No further questions, your Worship,' said the gymnast, bopping up and sitting down in one continuous movement.

'Any questions for the witness, Mr. Kowolski?'

'Sir,' said Kolowski standing up, taking off his glasses and pointing them at Jeanie.

'You say that Mr. Dean had been drinking?'

'Yes.'

'How do you know he had been drinking before you arrived home?'

'I – I saw the bottle on the table. It was half empty.'

'That does not mean that he had drunk the other half, does it?' No reply. Jeanie did not know what to say.

'You said that Mr. Dean hit your head against the wall. How many times did he do this?'

'I don't know.'

'Come, come, Mrs. Dean. Surely it is not too difficult to remember whether it was once, a couple of times, ten times?'

'I don't know.' How on earth could she be expected to have stood there counting?

'What do you have hanging against the wall next to the front door?'

She thought for a moment, then said, 'A hanging plant on the one side and a painting on the other.'

'You said that you were trying to get out of the front door –'

'I –' Jeanie interrupted him, wondering why the prosecutor did not say anything. The man was twisting the story.

'Don't interrupt, please Mrs. Dean,' he said rudely. 'You are here to answer questions, nothing else. Was it possible that you might have slipped, as I noticed you did in the court earlier, and bumped your head against the plant or painting?' 'That did not happen.'

'But was it possible?'

'Maybe.' The murmur which went up from the spectators told her that she must have said the wrong thing. Kowolski looked satisfied.

'What kind of work do you do, Mrs Dean?'

'I'm a district midwife.'

'Does that mean that you often have to go out alone on calls at night?' 'Yes.'

'Where do you live?'

'In Elsies River.'

'Would you say that Elsies River is a rough place?'

'Yes.'

'And you are not afraid to go out at night, unaccompanied?'

'It is my job.'

'Answer the question. We realise it is your job, but are you afraid when you go out alone at night?'

Fearing that the people, obviously used to court hearings, would show displeasure at her answer, Jeanie remained silent.

'Did you hear my question?'

She had no more words left. Surely they know there is a difference, she thought, becoming angry at the insistence of the man.

'I ask the court to note that the witness refuses to answer the question,' said Kowolski.

'Did Mr. Dean use any weapon?' he continued.

'No.'

'Are you alleging that he broke your hand and cut your scalp without using a weapon?'

'Yes.' Someone giggled.

'I believe that you recently spent a week away from home without your husband, Mrs. Dean.' Why did the prosecutor not tell the man that he was wasting time?

'Yes, I went on a holiday.'

'With your husband's knowledge and consent?'

'No, he did not know that I was going.'

'And you stayed away for a whole week?'

'Yes.'

'Were you afraid, then?'

'No'. Another ooh from the hushed audience.

'Would you agree that leaving your husband without his knowing where you were caused him some worry?' 'Yes.' What else could she say?

'Would you, with your experience of human nature, agree that a man can become very upset and angry out of worry when his wife goes away for a whole week without letting him know where she is and that she is safe?' No reply. Jeanie knew that to confirm this would be damning.

'I put it to you, Mrs. Dean, that you have been taunting your husband with totally unreasonable demands and actions. That he responded because of the extreme provocation you have subjected him to.'

Silence. This was why they call it cross-examination, went through Jeanie's head, looking at the lawyer who looked crossly at her.

'I have no further questions for the witness, your Worship,' Mr. Kowolski said with a victorious smirk.

'Re-examination, Mr. Prosecutor?' asked the magistrate.

'I have no further questions to ask, Sir. That is the end of the State's case,' the prosecutor said disinterestedly.

Jeanie did not hear the words 'You may step down now' and was quite surprised when the magistrate suddenly said, while rising, 'The court will adjourn for ten minutes,' and walked out while everyone scrambled to their feet.

Everybody seemed to know court procedure, except Jeanie, who sat alone and bewildered, still in the witness box. As soon as the magistrate was out of the door, the other people started talking with each other. They left the court room in groups. Everybody seemed to have somebody to tell their opinions to.

Jeanie remained standing in the witness box, not knowing what to do.

Eventually she realised that she could also go outside if she wanted to. Gregory had been taken down the steps and the only other person still in the room was the kindly old man, who stood looking at her. Gingerly she stepped down from the witness stand.

## Chapter 31

She decided it would be easier to stay in the court room. She felt cold and the hunger pangs were now really getting to her. She went to sit down in the same seat she had been sitting on earlier and bent forward in despondency. Tears started down her cheeks again and she bent her head down low, in case someone should come back into the room and see her cry. It all became too much for her.

The embarrassment she had been through that fateful night, weeks ago, was still excruciating.

Her ears and cheeks went red as she remembered herself crawling to the back door, then running out. She remembered the blood streaming down her face and onto her torn blouse, which she pulled closer to cover her exposed breast as she ran.

So frightened had she been this time that she had not even thought of taking the car. She did not have the keys with her anyway. She had just kept running, knowing that people were staring at her. Down the road, around the corner, right at the stop street, over the field she had run, looking back every few metres to see if Gregory was not following her. She ran for more than fifteen minutes, and her lungs had been aching, and she almost collapsed when she finally made it to the police station, and into the charge office.

Not knowing what she should do, she had gone to sit on a bench in a corner. There must have been about six other people there, all talking loudly, waiting their turn. She had sat there quietly, not knowing what to do, aching all over, blood pouring down through her hair onto her blouse, wiping her face now and then with the bottom edge of her blouse.

A big uniformed policeman on the other side of the grill eventually called her to the desk. Sobbingly she had tried to tell her story to him. All she remembered, very clearly, was his guarded look as he kept saying to her, over and over again, 'The police do not get involved in matters of a domestic nature. This is a civil matter. You must go and see your lawyer.'

Too dazed to make any sense of it all, Jeanie had gone back to her seat and just sat there. She must have been sitting in the same place for hours, for it was by then quite dark and she was still being ignored.

Eventually, perhaps because of what they thought was her stubbornness, the staff sergeant, who had just come on duty, told one of the officers to take a statement from Jeanie. By this time the blood on her head had coagulated and had formed a hard crust on her head. The weight of the blood had given her a pounding headache. It had started as a distant pain and had increasingly become worse. She did not then realise that her hand was broken because the pain in her hand had been minor compared to the pain in her head and when she breathed.

Someone must have realised I needed medical attention, Jeanie now thought, for someone had made sure that she be escorted to the hospital. It was the first time in her life that she'd travelled in the back of a police van.

But it was not to be the last time, as she was soon to know.

The junior police officer who had taken her there was kindlier. Jeanie had told him about her fear of going home and he agreed that, before he knocked off work the next morning, he would return and take her back to the police station.

All these memories came flooding back as the distraught woman sat outside the court room, convinced that the whole thing would backfire in her face. If Gregory walked away from court without reprimand or punishment, she feared for her life, for then he would have a licence to do precisely what he wanted to do with her.

She sat there crying quietly, not wanting to be heard, swallowing her sobs with shaking shoulders and trembling body.

By the time the court resumed, Jeanie had managed to stop crying and she waited, listlessly, convinced that there was no hope.

A strange thing happened when Gregory and his lawyer came into the court room.

Turning her head towards Gregory, she caught his eyes and an electric shock went down her spine. In some weird spiritual moment, an inner connection happened with the man. Between those two people who had, during the seven years of their marriage, tried to rent from each other every last iota of self-respect, like brother and sister they had become practised at inventing the most ingenious ways of tearing each other apart.

Yet in that moment, looking into Gregory's pained eyes, Jeanie felt his innermost fear, as if she could see right down into the very depths of his soul. She saw a small, frightened little boy, afraid of the future. She connected with his loneliness, his helplessness. Years of intimacy and deep knowledge of each other, having bred hatred, loathing, disrespect, had also, in some inexplicable way, given them a knowledge of each other which far exceeded the limitations of their physical experience and senses.

She saw very clearly that Gregory was a victim of circumstances, just as she was. And she also knew that there was no way that she would want to spend the rest of her life with the man, for his life was his life, and that it was not her responsibility to sort it out for him. This gave her immense relief from all the cultural and religious burdens which she had been carrying, which had up to then prevented her from leaving the man. She was not responsible for his life. The realisation gave her peace, no matter what the outcome of today might be.

Gregory was not called as a witness and the summing up which followed almost put Jeanie to sleep, she was so tired.

'What we are faced with here, your Worship, is the old problem which faced King Solomon,' she heard Kowolski say as she closed her eyes. 'Who is to be believed when there is no evidence corroborating either story? My humble submission is that my client is innocent. Or at most, should the Court find that he did inflict certain injuries on the complainant, that he was responding to immense provocation. The complainant's own admission is that she deserted him for a whole week before the incident. He is extremely sorry for what happened when she got home, but he was very worried for her safety while she was gone and what happened that afternoon was a result of her taunting him. He had acted without criminal intent and is sorry for what happened, which was totally out of character for him.'

'The complainant admitted that the accused used no weapon. In fact, the very essence of this case is in dire question. The Court would remember that Mrs. Dean declined to say anything when questioned about the possibility, the strong possibility, that she could have tripped and injured herself against one of the attachments on the wall.'

'My submission –' and on and on and on, until Jeanie stopped listening altogether, resigned that she had blown everything.

The magistrate eventually had his turn after the prosecutor again declined to say anything. If I ever have any say in these matters, thought Jeanie, I will make sure that all cases involving women are prosecuted by women.

'Will the accused please stand.' So, Gregory did.

Looking at Gregory, the magistrate continued, 'The court has heard the submissions made on your behalf by your legal representative. It is obvious that no weapon was used, and the charge of Grievous Bodily Harm can therefore not be sustained,' and Jeanie bowed her head. This is the last time I ever try to ask the law for protection, she thought.

The magistrate continued. 'The court finds the accused guilty of the lesser charge of Common Assault.' Jeanie turned to look at the prosecutor, to see whether he would say anything. What did this mean? What was the meaning of a lesser charge? She had heard the word guilty, but guilty of what?

Mr. Kowolski stood up and this confused Jeanie even more. He went on about his client's character and how any action on his part was out of character. He told the court about Gregory's blameless criminal history, about his important job as a Chartered Accountant, a steady, hardworking person.

'For Mr .Dean to be incarcerated,' he ended, 'for him to serve a prison sentence would be, to borrow a French term, a catastrophe for not only himself, but for his whole family who are dependent upon him. He is bound to lose his job and I accordingly submit that the best sentence in the circumstances would be for him to be given a warning by the court, for he is genuinely sorry for this mishap.'

Jeanie wished that South Africa had retained the jury system, for to her it seemed so unfair that a single man should be able to make a decision which could have far reaching consequences. She did not quite know what Kowolski meant, but if Gregory should escape punishment, her life would be in danger.

She tried hard to understand the rest of the proceedings. The sentence was too complicated for her tired brain to work out. All she heard was '…suspended for two years.'

The court room emptied quickly after that. People filed out in pairs, with loud voices discussing weighty legal procedure. She saw Gregory and his lawyer shake hands before they, too, walked out.

The court bailiff was waiting for her to leave. She was the last person in the room, for even the prosecutor had left with Kowolski and Gregory, without a further word to her.

Slowly she walked towards the door. She peeped sheepishly into the corridor. Nobody was there. As she stepped through the doors, it dawned on Jeanie that the clerk of the court might be able to help her.

She turned back into the court room, where the old man was busy switching off the lights.

'Please, will you tell me something?' she asked him.

'Yes, my dear?'

'You were in the court and heard what happened, didn't you?'

'Yes, I was there.'

'Would you mind explaining to me what happens now?'

'Do you mean, what happens with your husband?'

'Yes, please.'

'Well, I don't think he will be violent towards you for a very long time, if ever again. I have been around for many years and I recognise a man when he is sorry. Your husband does not look a bad lad and I know that he has learnt his lesson.'

'But what happens if he hits me again?', this being the important part of it all.

'He got a three-month jail sentence. But he will not need to go to jail. Not yet.' Jeanie's heart sank. He is free to do anything with me that he wants to do. He will definitely kill me now, she thought while she stared at the man in total helplessness.

'If he should touch you again, his lawyer will not be able to do much for him, because there is an interdict out against him. He cannot go near you ever again. You will be able to report him to the police immediately he comes within 20 metres of you,' he continued, trying to console her.

'What's an interdict? How does it look?'

'It's a document with the court's seal on it,' he explained patiently. 'It will be delivered to you and it will give you the right to charge him immediately if he breaks the rules of the court order which will be written on it.' How safe would a piece of paper keep me at midnight after some drinks, Jeanie wondered, but she did not say this to the kind man.

'I can't go back home because I know that another argument will start up,' she said. 'Do you think the police will help me, I mean, do you think they will go with me to fetch my things?'

Before she had finished her question, she saw him shake his head. Her disappointment must have shown on her face, for he very gently said next, 'Tell you what I'll do. Come to my office on the first floor, first door on the right, in fifteen minutes' time. I will try to find a court policeman and ask him to go home with you, yes?'

She felt better and thanked him. Not only for the help which he was offering, but also for the support he had unknowingly given her earlier, which had meant so much to her, but which he definitely did not realise.

More confidently now, Jeanie strode out of the court room. As she crossed the passage, she saw an open stretch of grass through the big windows. She decided to go and sit in the sun for a few minutes.

The warmth of the sun and the silence outside, silence of a different kind, not as depressing and subdued as inside the courthouse, was a relief.

## Chapter 32

Slowly Jeanie strode over the grass verge and threw her handbag down.

As she was folding her skirt around her knees to sit down, she heard, as if her repetitive daydream over the last few months had come true, 'Hello, there, nursie!'

It could not possible be his voice, she thought, afraid to look around in case it turned out to be an illusion.

But she could not help doing this and, yes, it was he.

He walked along over the grass towards her with the same, easy, long strides which she remembered from that first meeting. But this time he did not look quite so Afrikaans or like the farmer she had taken him to be. He was dressed in a dark blue suit and carrying a briefcase. Please don't let him be a lawyer, flashed through her mind. She'd had enough of lawyers for one day.

Her heart pounded as he stopped in front of her. She squinted up at the big man and, again, was impressed by the gold flakes on his head sparkling in the sun behind him.

'How are you, my mystery nurse?' he asked with laughter in his voice. His smile disappeared as he looked down at Jeanie and he continued, with concern, 'My, but you do look tired. Are you ill?'

Jeanie felt immediately embarrassed and, instinctively, she looked down at the wide, floral skirt she was wearing, bloodstains still visible amongst the flowers, although she had tried so hard to wash them down in the hospital toilet and after that, again and again. The outsized sweater which she loved looked creased. She felt unkempt. She lifted her arm and tried to flatten her hair in an awkward movement. She did not know what to say and looked up at him pitifully.

'Would you like to –' He did not get a chance to finish his sentence, and turned his head, following Jeanie's gaze, for she had momentarily looked away from him. Behind him the clerk of the court had appeared and was waiving his hand towards her.

Not sure whether to be relieved or distressed about the interruption, Jeanie said, 'Sorry, but I'm afraid I have to go.'

She was in such a rush that she did not pause to take the hand which he was offering to her to help her stand up. She jumped up and, grabbing her bag, ran towards the clerk of the court, without saying goodbye. She could have kicked herself afterwards.

'This is Sergeant Brown,' the clerk introduced the tall young man standing next to him. 'He has kindly agreed to take you to your home. But don't delay him too long, because he will be going outside his area and he is merely doing us a favour,' he said.

The policeman did not look at all like a policeman. He was wearing faded blue jeans and a black sweater and black leather jacket. She greeted him and noticed his open, clean smile, which reassured her.

As she strolled away with the policeman she glanced back. The Afrikaner was gone.

What a fool I am, she thought. She had been longing for the day when she might meet him again. Now it had happened and she had not even asked his name. If only she had had the presence of mind to do that.

The sun seemed to have gone dimmer now and Jeanie was convinced that there was nothing that she would ever again be able to do right. She walked besides the policeman, who did not speak with her, but merely strolled slowly towards the car park.

Her tired mind did not allow her much thinking as they drove along. The policeman, who was concentrating on the road, softly whistling an off-key tune, looked completely unafraid and relaxed. He gave her confidence. He was so assured and calm and this helped her to feel better.

'O my,' she suddenly realised. 'I do not have a key to the front door!' anxiously looking at him.

'Well, that should not present too big a problem,' he said calmly. 'Perhaps a window might be open, then you can climb through and open the front door from the inside.'

When they took the turn into Green Street where she lived, she immediately saw Gregory's Volvo parked in the driveway.

She had hoped he would not be there.

'That's the house, there,' she pointed, 'where the green Volvo is parked.' Without a word he easily pulled the police car into the driveway and parked behind Gregory's car.

She waited nervously for him to get out of the car and walk around it, so that she could walk with him to the door. She looked through the window at the side of the house as she passed it, but did not see Gregory anywhere.

The front door was open and Jeanie peeped through. The room was empty. 'Please come inside and sit down,' she almost pleaded with the policeman, and he followed her in with a quiet smile.

She walked through the inter leading door, through the short passage and, just as she was about to pass the kitchen, she saw Gregory standing at the kitchen sink, drinking a glass of water.

'I've come to fetch my clothes,' she said hurriedly.

'What do you want your clothes for. And don't you know how to greet?' he said, nastily.

'I've decided to leave. I cannot go on living with you anymore,' she said, trying to keep the tenseness out of her voice and eyes.

'And where do you think you're going to? Back to your w'horehouse in Jo'burg?'

She did not answer and slowly stepped back into the passage, reversing towards the sitting room where she knew she would be safe. He came striding purposefully towards her.

'And who do we have here!' His voice went louder as he saw the policeman, who was standing up, facing him.

What do I do now, Jeanie wondered. She was not sure whether to go through a formal introduction. It was all so silly.

She was saved by Sergeant Brown, who said, 'I'm a policeman. I have come to help your wife to take her things away.'

'Oh,' was all he could say, temporarily lost for words, but immediately followed with sarcasm: 'What does she want a policeman for? Take your things,' to Jeanie 'and go back into the street where you belong. That is where you have always wanted to be anyway.'

Jeanie stood, unable to move, and he continued, 'So? Expected trouble, did you? Well, why the hell don't you go and take your things and get out? You make me sick!'

This moved her mind back into gear. 'I would like to take my books and music as well, and fetch some kitchen things tomorrow –.' She wanted to get what she could out of him while the policeman was there to protect her.

The look she got from him froze her up completely. 'You want to do what? Listen, you slut,' his voice was now again rising and she saw the veins stand out on his temples as he tried to control himself. He barely glanced at the policeman, who was standing quietly, watching him.

'You were quite happy to walk out and leave your things here. If you don't want the home I am giving you, then stay without it. The things in this house belong to me, until a court tells me otherwise. So run to court again.'

His look made her blood curl. 'and no policeman can help you there!' he said, giving the policeman a dark look. 'I know my rights, too. Now just take your clothes and get out. You've got five minutes.'

The policeman gave a shrug as she glanced at him, and she knew that there was no sense in pushing the matter further.

Fear renders protection impotent, Jeanie thought as she walked back through the passage, leaving the two men sizing each other up. She went into the bedroom and lifted a big, empty case from the top of the wardrobe. She put it on the bed and opened the dressing table drawer. She was in a daze and was trembling.

She went through the four drawers, opening and closing them senselessly, not taking any clothing out, not sure what she was doing. Without concentrating, she threw a pair of knickers into the empty case, went to the wardrobe, opened the doors and stood there for a minute in confusion. Then she turned back to the dressing table, opened the top drawer and closed it again. Fortunately, her eye caught her uniforms hanging in the corner of the room, behind the door. She knew she would need them, and put them in the case. One bedroom slipper was thrown in next, simply because she almost tripped over it. Next went in her midwifery bag and the book which was lying on the bedside cabinet.

Without quite knowing the reason for what she did next, Jeanie picked up the half empty case and walked out of the bedroom into the spare room. As she was about to step inside, Gregory's voice, right behind her, made her jump. 'You don't want anything in there. I told you, you had five minutes. Are you deaf, woman?'

He was becoming really angry now, she knew. He made a grab for the case which she was holding in her right hand. She pulled back. Stepping aside, he gave her a push into the passage, towards the sitting room, where she could see the policeman. As she passed the bedroom, she saw her nursing shoes on the floor inside the door and quickly grabbed them, knowing he would not touch her with the policeman's eyes on them.

'I'm ready,' she said breathlessly to the policeman as she came into the front room.

He looked at her quietly, then took the case from her and gently took the shoes and case from her hand.

Gregory came in. He stood next to her, staring at the policeman, daring him to say something. Jeanie pushed through them, out onto the verandah.

Sergeant Brown opened the passenger door of the police car for her and put the case and her shoes on the back seat and closed the door.

Gregory stood with folded arms watching them and as the policeman started up the car, turned back into the house and slammed the door shut behind him.

Gratefully she later climbed into the yet unknown and uncomfortable little bed in the back room in the back yard of her friend Ellen.

Too tired to keep her eyes open for long, she fell into a deep sleep while the sun put another day to sleep to keep her company in her dreams.

# Chapter 33

'Jeanie, phone!' It sounded far away and slowly drew her up from a fitful sleep.

She was once again surprised to open her eyes onto a cooker on a table in the corner, where her dressing table should have been. The smell of last night's fish and chips still floated around in the narrow, single roomed little servant's room she now lived in.

It took her a few seconds to shake off the muffled effects of sleep before she called out 'Ok, coming,' her voice travelling through the open window across the small paved back yard to her friend who was standing in the backdoor to the big house.

She grabbed her dressing gown and, without bothering to find slippers, ran out, wrapping the gown around her. She went through the kitchen door and walked across the orange and white Italian tiles into the foyer between the dining room and sitting room in her friend's big house.

'Hello,' she said into the receiver, then cleared her throat, which was still groggy with sleep.

'Jeanie?' a woman's high-pitched voice, unfamiliar to Jeanie.

'Yes?'

'It's Cynthia. Zogi used to share the house with us, remember me?' Jeanie was now wide awake.

'O, hi, Cynthia. How did you get hold of me?' curious to know why Cynthia should want to phone her after so many years.

'Your husband didn't want to tell me where you were,' Cynthia explained.

'So, I phoned your headquarters and pretended to be an old patient of yours. They gave me your number.'

'O yeah?'

'Zogi asked me to phone you,' Cynthia said.

'Zogi?' Jeanie could not understand where all this was leading to.

'Yes. She's in Valkenberg.'

'O my God! What's she doing there?' Valkenberg Asylum as it was called, was where the worst of psychiatric cases were admitted.

'I don't know. A nurse phoned me. Said Zogi said I must contact you.'

Too shocked to respond, Jeanie stood there with the phone in her hand.

'You still there, Jeanie?'

'Yea, I'm here,' said Jeanie, all thoughts of her own dilemma suspended in her concern for Zogi. 'Do you know what she's in Valkenberg for, Cynthia?'

'No, I don't know why she's there, Jeanie. I haven't been to see her. She asked for you.'

'What did the nurse say, how is she?'

'Apparently, she's very depressed. They told me she's getting no visits from her family.'

'How long has she been there, do you know?' Johannesburg is a long way from Cape Town and how on earth did Zogi get here in her state, went through Jeanie's mind.

'I've got no idea, Jeanie. You going to see her?'

'Yes, I'll arrange it.' Jeanie was frowning deeply, her full lips puckered as she bit into the inside of her cheek. 'Got a phone number for me, please Cynthia?'

'No. I didn't get a number. Let me know how she is, will you?' said Cynthia, in a hurry to get off the phone.

'Ya. I'll let you know. Thanks for letting me know, Cynthia,' Jeanie said, replacing the receiver slowly. She stood there, deep in thought for a few moments. She was surprised, but also pleased, that Zogi had called for her. Jeanie was already trying to re-arrange her work so she could see Zogi that afternoon.

Ellen, Jeanie's friend and landlady, had come outside. 'Is something wrong, Jeanie,' she asked from behind Jeanie, seeing her standing there, not moving. Jeanie turned her head, not moving, a puzzled look on her face.

'Come, let's have a cup of coffee,' Ellen said, walking past Jeanie into the kitchen, and Jeanie followed her.

'Hey, what's wrong?' Ellen said with concern as she filled the kettle. 'Want to talk about it? It's Gregory again, isn't it?'

'No, not him,' answered Jeanie, reluctant to talk about Zogi, whom Ellen did not know. Strange how separated my friends are from each other, Jeanie thought. There are those of us who are so close because we share the same political views and action, I suppose. Those who are not involved, even family, don't know what we do or who our friends are. What a double life I lead, she thought as she stared up at Ellen who was carefully making the coffee.

'Meant to tell you,' Ellen continued, 'Greg was here last night again. You were out.'

'Oh no, not again,' Jeanie mumbled through a tight jaw, sitting with elbows on the table, cupped right palm supporting her head.

'Yes. He must've been drunk. Kept banging on your door 'till I came out. He shouted the most horrible things about you.'

This Jeanie could have done without. Here it goes again, she thought.

'What did Charles say?' Charles was a kind, quiet man, Ellen's husband.

'Luckily Charles wasn't home. When Greg did it last week, Charles said to tell you it can't go on this way. Last night was the third time, Jeanie. I wish I could do something for you, but you know how Charles is. It does worry one because all the neighbours could hear.'

Jeanie's heart sank. Now she had left him, Gregory was into a different kind of aggression.

'He knows he can't beat me up anymore. But he's out to make things more difficult for me,' she said. 'Remember, I told you, the last people I was living with in Crawford also asked me to go because he kept coming to the house to cause a scene every other night during the two weeks I was there?'

'But Jeanie, you have a restraining order out against him, why don't you report him to the police?'

Why don't I? Jeanie did not have enough faith in the law, and she could not explain to Ellen the nightmare experience of going back to court. She would avoid that at all costs.

'At least it seems as if he is not going to get physical,' she said weakly, not sure that she believed what she was saying.

'I don't know, Jeanie. I don't trust that man. I don't think he has any respect for the law. But what can I do, Jeanie? If Charles should hear what happened here last night, he won't like it.' How will he find out if you don't tell him, Jeanie thought, but said nothing. There was nothing to say.

She knew, though, what was coming.

'Anyway,' continued Ellen, 'I think we should work this out between us, as women, and not get the men involved.' She stayed quiet for a moment, expectantly. Jeanie did not respond other than to raise her eyebrows expectantly.

'So I think it will be best for all of us if you find another place, Jeanie.' Oh my God, here it comes, thought Jeanie, too distressed to give any reply.

'I thought about it since last night,' Ellen added quickly, 'and I remembered that a lady I know at aerobic classes said she has a spare room in one of her servant's quarters. If you like, I'll phone her. I'm sure she'll help you out if she knows we're friends.' Jeanie could see the relief on Ellen's face, now that she had said it all.

Jeanie felt bone tired with frustration. What must be, must be, she thought, resigned. She had made her decision and she had no intention of going back to Gregory.

'That's kind of you, Ellen. Yes, please, give her a ring for me, will you? I'll check with you when I get back. In the meantime, I'll look out for myself as well.'

'Thanks for taking me in, Ellen,' she said as she stood up, now in a hurry to get out of Ellen's house to her little room at the back. 'Tell Charles that I really appreciate it, will you?' she said with a forced smile on her face, not looking at Ellen, coffee forgotten.

She was in a hurry to get to Valkenberg hospital and decided to go straight there, instead of phoning first. She also could not use Ellen's telephone as the arrangement was that she would not use it for outgoing calls. Ellen and Charles had agreed to take her district calls, and she was grateful for this.

She had a quick shower. This meant walking out of her little room to the other side of the yard, where the single shower room was, between her room and the gardener's shack.

She made the little bed methodically after she had changed into her uniform, and packed her few belongings back into her single case. She realised how strong she had become since that time when she had walked out of her house, and Gregory's life, with a single half-empty suitcase.

Jeanie was determined not to contact Gregory or to go begging for the things she had left behind. This surprised her. She felt relief rather than worry about the life she had left behind. The freedom from fear that she had enjoyed since leaving Gregory helped her to cope with the way her life had changed and the contrast of her life now.

Working with her poor patients reminded her, every day, how lucky she was. She knew that she at least had a chance to get out of the second-grade existence she was in, for she still had her job and had prospects of a better life ahead. But for most of the poor people she worked with there is just a bleak future of sameness and very little space for dreams of a better life.

This reminded Jeanie of her mother. Her mind went back to the time when she accompanied her mother to Pastor Cowley's house years ago.

She remembered that their rent had not been paid for five months and eviction loomed. Her mum was terribly worried. Her last resort was Pastor Cowley.

Pastor Cowley knew their family well: that dad had died, leaving mum with nine children to see through school and college, something almost unachievable for a non-white family in apartheid South Africa in the nineteen fifties.

He also knew that hand-outs from the church and hand-downs from family were keeping them going, while mum carried on working at the local factory as a machinist. And above all, stubborn woman that she was, he knew that she would not even consider adoption or fostering, despite continuous advice from everybody in authority.

When mum tiredly dragged herself up the steps of his immense, curved, marble front porch on that hot Sunday afternoon, Jeanie could see from the look on his face that the charitable Pastor Cowley felt a mixed emotion of sorrow at the sight of such suffering, but also anger at the pig-headedness of the woman. Or that's what Jeanie had thought he thought. At age thirteen Jeanie knew everything about life and people.

Jeanie saw him close his Sunday Times and stand up with military politeness and attention for her mum to sit down. He did not greet Jeanie – just a cursory glance – and Jeanie wondered (still to today) why Mum spoke of him as if he were God's Mr. Nice.

It took her a cup of tea, a cup of tears and a long time to tell him her latest woe. Pastor kept glancing at Jeanie. It was obvious to her that he could not understand why Jeanie was there. Jeanie wondered too, for she knew that her mum was wasting her time, that the plea would get the usual 'I wish there was something I could do for you' response.

Jeanie had sat half listening, lost in her own thoughts. The coolness and cleanliness of Pastor Cowley's house fascinated her. The birds were twittering in the lazy midday heat and she became intoxicated with the lovely smells and tranquillity of the place. So different from the confusion of their rowdy little wooden house on the wrong side of the railway bridge!

Jeanie remembered how she had came to her senses and jumped up when Mum was already standing up. Pastor had his hand under her elbow, saying, in his kindest voice:

'Don't worry, sister. In our Father's house are many mansions, which He has gone to prepare for us.'

On her way down the steps Jeanie turned and saw Pastor Cowley pouring fresh, cold orange juice into a sparkling glass.

The sound of crackling ice in a cool drink on a hot day still reminded her of the earthly mansion which they had lost, and which her dear ma was still waiting for 44 years later, when she died in her little backroom in someone else's rented flat on a dilapidated council estate.

She did, though, see all of us through high school, mused Jeanie as she rushed through her duties that morning, wanting to get to the hospital to see Zogi as soon as she could. She also saw two of us through nursing college, one through midwifery training, three through teaching college and one of us through law school.

She also gave us the strength and conviction to fight for freedom from oppression and sacrifice our own wellbeing for others, and that was the heritage Jeanie was most proud about.

Her nursing duties were soon over that morning, and she headed for Valkenberg hospital. Zogi's baby might be born by now. I hope everything went well for her, thought Jeanie, perhaps we could even arrange to live together with the baby! The thought made her feel exhilarated and her mind immediately went into exciting plans for how this could happen.

She arrived at the hospital at 3 o'clock that fateful Wednesday afternoon.

## Chapter 34

The flat, white building with its small, barred windows stood behind a 4-metre fence, camouflaging the suffering inside under sterile orderliness. A few people were sitting on benches in the sun, looking with disinterest at Jeanie as she walked towards the large wooden doors, still wearing her blue district nurse's uniform.

It took about three minutes for Jeanie to hear the jingling of a heavy bunch of keys on the other side of the heavy door after she had rang the bell. The smiling young nurse with a cheeky nose was not what Jeanie had expected.

'Can I help you?' said the nurse, with twinkling blue eyes.

'Yes, please. May I come inside?'

'Visiting hours are almost over, I'm afraid,' said the nurse, standing aside to allow Jeanie to pass by her into the cold, gloomy passage.

'I've come to see one of your patients.' The nurse had turned to lock the heavy outside doors and Jeanie spoke into her back.

'Who?' the nurse asked, turning to Jeanie.

'Zogi Pillay,' Jeanie said, hoping that Zogi had used her father's name this time. People, especially those politically involved, used so many different surnames, mostly to avoid detection by the police. Zogi might have chosen any one of the half dozen names she had used, which had got her out of many a scrap.

'This is actually the men's section,' said the nurse, but continued, helpfully, 'Come with me. I'll show you where the women are.'

Together they walked along the long corridors on shining vinyl floors. They passed a tall, tired looking man, in his own little world, with deep concentration methodically pulling a long mop back and forth across a small section of the spotless floor.

The depressive atmosphere of the place became heavier as they walked deeper into the maze of corridors in the big building. Not much sun was coming through the high windows of the corridor, all barred up with black iron bars. A nauseating smell of carbolic soap and dettol was hanging heavily over their heads and, somewhere, far away, from the bowels of the so-called sanctuary, Jeanie could hear the hysterical scream of some dissatisfied soul.

The nurse took her directly to the office of the duty nursing Sister on the other side of the building. After saying who Jeanie wanted to see, she left them, the permanent smile of a job well done still on her contented young face.

The Sister, the second most senior nurse in the hospital hierarchy, very serious and possibly in her fifties, looked at Jeanie for a moment and said, 'Oh yes. You must be her friend. She keeps asking for you. Would you mind sitting down for a moment? Your name is Jeanie Dean, isn't it?' as she suddenly realised that she might have made an assumption from the nurses' uniform, as she had not been given a name. When Jeanie nodded, she continued, 'I'd like to talk with you first, nurse Dean.'

Jeanie, who really could not wait to see Zogi, did not really want to sit down, but she did so reluctantly on the hard seat with its upright arms which the Sister pushed towards her.

'I'm Sister Jones.' The lady introduced herself as she walked around the desk to sit with her back to the window, next to Jeanie. 'Zogi was admitted about four weeks ago.'

'Is her baby born yet?' was Jeanie's main concern.

'Yes, a girl. She's two days old,' came the happy news, said by the woman in a very businesslike manner. 'She had an uncomplicated delivery,' continued Sister Jones, pausing for a moment as she reached over on her desk for a blue folder. She opened it and looked up at Jeanie after turning a page. 'Her uncle brought her here. Do you know her family?'

'I've met Zogi's mum and dad,' Jeanie said. 'Don't know them very well, though. I heard that her father died recently, but I'm not sure how her mum is.'

'It was a friend of hers who insisted she be admitted, he told me himself, because he was with the uncle when Zogi was brought in.' She went quiet for a while, studying the file. 'I see here that she had apparently taken an overdose of sleeping tablets.'

Jeanie took in a sharp breath, looking fixedly at the woman's bent head, wondering what was to follow.

'Apparently she had been suicidal for a while, the doctor's letter says here, since she arrived back from Jo'burg,' she said with bent head, still reading from the folder.

Jeanie hid her shock as the nurse looked up at her, frowning slightly, her dark brown eyes going cloudy behind heavy framed glasses. 'Her mother went overseas the next day and nobody has been to visit Zogi since.' Jeanie sat there, her huge eyes showing her deep feeling for her lonely friend. 'When do you think Zogi can leave the hospital?' she asked the nurse, when the other went into her own thoughts for a while.

'She's very depressed and is receiving quite heavy medication still,' came the reply. 'It might have been considered to send her home had her parents been here, but we cannot do that until we know that she has someone to look after her properly.'

'I…,' Jeanie started to say, then immediately changed her mind. It would be premature to offer to take Zogi in, when she, herself, did not know where she might be within the next week or so.

'What do you want me to do?' she asked instead.

'Possibly all you could do, right now, is to try and visit Zogi regularly. She obviously thinks a lot of you and is very close to you. Your being around will help her improvement very much.' With this, the Sister stood up and, bending down with pencil perched in her left hand, she said, 'Perhaps you would give us your phone number, in case we need to call you. Or, perhaps, when we have worked out where she can go when discharged from here.'

'Sure,' said Jeanie, giving her Ellen's telephone number, but not bothering to say that she might herself not be living there for long.

A wise decision, as things stand right now, Jeanie thought.

The Sister scribbled down the number and walked past Jeanie to the door. 'Come, I'll show you where she is.'

At last! Excitedly Jeanie followed the nurse, almost running to keep up with her. They entered a long dormitory and walked between two rows of about twenty single beds on each side, neatly made up and with a locker between each bed. On the far side of the room Jeanie saw her friend sitting with her hands resting in her lap, her long hair hanging untidily over her shoulders and down onto the front of the oversized white hospital gown she was wearing.

The only other person in the room was an old woman, who was sitting next to the long centre table near Zogi's bed, her toothless jaws moving up and down rhythmically as she opened and closed her mouth, chewing her tongue as if it were a tasty piece of meat.

'She's not well today,' she winked up at Jeanie, lifting the forefinger of her left hand to her mouth, while rolling her eyes up in the direction of the Sister, seemingly passing on a big secret. Head bent forward, staring at her hands, Zogi did not see Jeanie until they were standing next to her. Her listless hazel eyes transformed. They lit up and the screen of disinterest lifted from them as she saw and recognised her friend. Pleasure filled her face.

'Ah, knew you'd be good for her,' the Sister said, pleased that she had started this reunion. She walked away from them, pressing Zogi lightly on her thin shoulder.

Unsteadily Zogi stood up, her arms extended. Jeanie went right into them and, swinging her arms around Zogi's thin frame, and gave her a long, warm hug.

The old lady, scratching her scalp under untidy grey hair, looked up at the two of them intently, responding to the warmth which flowed from the younger women with a broad grin.

'You'd better get out of here so I can fatten you up,' were the first words Jeanie said to her friend as Zogi, already tired from just standing up briefly, sank into the chair next to the bed.

'I'm so happy you came, my sissie' she said, hanging onto Jeanie's hand as Jeanie sat down on the edge of the bed.

'So you're a mother, hey!' Jeanie laughed, stroking her friend's soft hair. Her hair felt sticky and in dire need of a wash.

Zogi's eyes went dark as she abruptly changed the subject. 'Howzit Jeanie? Greg been treating you better?'

Knowing Zogi so well, Jeanie realised that the subject of the baby must be causing her distress. She readily went along with her friend's need to let it wait. 'Not too well, but I'll manage. I've left Greg,' keenly watching Zogi's reaction. It was as expected:

'I'm glad,' Zogi said. 'You should have done that years ago.'

Jeanie could not help smiling at the girl's honesty. 'It was a real big bang up. A few weeks ago. It's hard, at the moment, because I'm not sure where I'll be staying until I find a permanent place, but I know that things will work out. I feel so free, Zogi.'

Zogi nodded in complete understanding. She sat looking at her friend with adoring eyes for a while, then a broad smile spread across her face as she said, 'And what happened with your secret lover?'

'What do you mean, secret lover?' It was Jeanie's turn to smile, knowing full well whom Zogi was talking about, but wanting to know how on earth she knew about the Afrikaner.

'Remember that night when we saw each other last?' Zogi asked, unable to keep the amusement from her voice.

'Yes, it was lovely. What about it?' Jeanie said guardedly.

'Jeanie, you really are so transparent for your 32 years. Any child could see that you were dreaming of someone that day. I'd hoped you'd tell me about it, but we had no time, did we?'

You're not only pretty, talented, educated, but also sharp, thought Jeanie without envy, as she replied, 'OK, you clever lady. Seeing you suspect so much, how about telling me about it?' and they both laughed.

At the thought of him, Jeanie's eyes grew softer. 'Zogi, I'm such a clot - ,' she started.

'Yeah, we all know that!' Zogi interrupted with a giggle.

'I'd been dreaming about the guy. Then, what do I do when I meet him?'

'You tell him "sorry, sir, I'm otherwise engaged",' came the reply with a girlish laugh.

'I did almost exactly that!' said Jeanie with a laugh. 'We got interrupted by more important things and I had to run away. And I left without telling him where to find me – that is, if he is interested in finding me, which I doubt after the way I looked when he saw me outside the courthouse.'

'Court? What were you doing at court, Jeanie?'

Not wanting to burden her with the sorry details of that horrible time, Jeanie just smiled and said 'I'll tell you about that sometime. Right now, we need to talk about you,' Jeanie said seriously. 'What on earth are you doing here, anyway, Zogi? You don't belong here.'

This time Zogi's face dropped. It took her a while to look Jeanie in the eye. 'Yes, Jeanie,' she said. 'I know that. But it was by far the safest place for me to be.' Softly, her voice heavy with pain.

Jeanie did not say a word, waiting for Zogi to continue, which she did, after another pause, while she stared past the head of the now sleeping old woman.

'I wish I had a mother who understood me better, Jeanie. I miss my dad so much. At least I could talk with him. Mum is so ... so, I don't know. She has these social standards which twist my gut,' she said, closing her eyes and drawing them together with her fingers, a frown on her face.

'What happened, Zogi?' asked Jeanie, instantly feeling Zogi's change of mood and her hurt.

'Jeanie, my mum has forced me into agreeing to have the baby adopted.' Zogi started crying softly.

'But you don't need to do what your mum tells you to do,' Jeanie reassured her. 'You know, in fact, you've always known, your own mind.'

'Yes. I would not have agreed if my mum had not fetched me in Hillbrow. I'd have coped, somehow, away from her.' Zogi wiped her nose on the big sleeve of her gown and looked up at her friend pleadingly. 'When I realised they wanted me home, I also thought my mum would accept the baby. But this did not happen.'

'Let's look at it this way,' Jeanie said, trying to force her friend's mind into a different direction. 'You've still got the baby, haven't you?'

'Yes,' said Zogi, her eyes brightening up for a brief second. 'Wanna see her, Jeanie?'

Jeanie nodded and, hand in hand, they walked out of the dormitory towards the nursery.

Remembering their walk to the nursery in the days to come, Jeanie felt sure that they had not been seen. She could not remember seeing any of the staff, nor any other person around as they stood in the passage, looking through the large windows at the three little cots inside the room.

'Guess which one,' said Zogi, looking up at Jeanie with pride.

'That's difficult -,' Jeanie began. But immediately, with a laugh, she pointed to the little black head on the far right. 'There she is!' as the baby at that moment opened close-set hazel eyes and looked straight at Jeanie.

'Wow, Zogi, she's beautiful,' Jeanie said, almost reverently, her eyes fixed on the perfect little body, fists tightly closed.

Zogi had gone quiet and Jeanie, feeling as sad, said, in a low voice, 'When are they coming to fetch her?'

'They said tomorrow morning. We're signing the papers together, then they're taking her away.'

'You mean they hope to sign the papers and take her away,' Jeanie said, almost without thinking. Their heads jerked towards each other, eyes opened wide.

The seed of a crazy plan had popped into their heads at the same time.

## Chapter 35

'We can do it!' whispered Zogi, in her excitement pinching Jeanie's arm. 'I've got a key to my parent's holiday home in Strandfontein. Nobody will think to look for you there …'

Jeanie was completely carried away. At long last her longing for a baby of her own would be satisfied.

The two friends went into action without further words. Also, without regard for consequences.

There was nobody in the passage. Jeanie stood at the door of the nursery, while Zogi slipped inside. Within a minute, and while a bell rang somewhere to signal the end of visiting time, Jeanie walked around the corner to the men's side of the building with the baby, cuddling the little girl warmly through a light blanket against her breast, holding the house key which had quickly passed from under Zogi's gown into her hand.

Zogo innocently, now smiling broadly, walked back into the dormitory, climbed straight into bed, hid her head and started dreaming of better days to come.

By the time Jeanie got to the outer door through which she had come just twenty minutes before, a stream of people was heading the same way. The door was open to let the visitors out and she simply followed the crowd of people, convinced that she had not been seen by any of the staff.

She did not attract any curious looks either. Fortunately, she was wearing her nurse's uniform and it must have looked like the most natural thing in the world for a nurse to be carrying a baby out of a hospital at four in the afternoon, Jeanie thought, for she was not stopped.

She had, as was not unusual, forgotten to lock the car doors and she drove out of the car park immediately after carefully placing the baby on the front passenger's seat, out of sight.

By the time she reached Goodwood Main Road to turn right and head back to Elsies River, her immediate plan was worked out. She dared not think too far ahead. All Jeanie knew was that she had what she had wanted for so many, many years. Her friend, no matter if she changed her mind within the next few weeks, had granted her the honour of having a baby all to herself.

What joy!

She drove along very slowly, keeping her eye on the still sleeping infant next to her on the seat. She could not have put into words her feelings. She felt elated and proud, riding high on adrenalin during those twenty minutes it took her to drive back to Ellen's house.

Before she turned the corner into Ellen's street, she stopped the car and transferred the baby onto the back seat. Then, silently praying that the infant would not attract attention, she threw her nursing cape over the sleeping baby.

Jeanie ran straight to the rear of the house, into her little room. She did not bother to take any of the few belongings which made up her houseware, taking only the few items of clothing and toiletries in the case. She rushed out, locking the door behind her.

Fortunately, Ellen answered the back door immediately.

Jeanie's smile was broad. 'I've found another place to stay, Ellen. Would you mind, just for a few days, taking calls for me?'

Ellen also smiled, in relief, and nodded. 'That was quick, Jeanie. I'm so glad.'

'I'll phone you. I'm not on duty, anyway, until Saturday morning, so there should not be any calls for a few days,' and with a 'thanks for everything, Ellen,' she rushed around the house, hardly hearing Ellen's goodbye.

'You're the best baby I've ever known,' whispered Jeanie over her shoulder as she backed out of the quiet cul-de-sac, carefully turning left and heading for the freeway. She dared not stop before she was well out of Ellen's district.

She could not resist to pull up under a tree and climb into the back seat before joining the freeway traffic. The little infant was sucking furiously away on its right thumb as Jeanie lifted it and held it reverently to her breast. The feeling of warmth and belonging which both of them had in that moment was to remain in Jeanie's memory for a long time.

'No matter how this turns out,' Jeanie whispered to the baby in wonderment as her extended forefinger was tightly gripped in the soft palm of a little pink hand, 'I belong to you and Zogi, and you to me and Zogi and all of us to each other. Forever,' she vowed, meaning every word of it.

She stopped at a supermarket to stock up with baby milk and disposable nappies. She popped into Woolworths in Claremont Main Road for a few hastily chosen baby clothes, then headed for the big holiday home of the Pillays in Strandfontein near the seaside.

The next twenty-four hours were the most beautiful Jeanie had known in years. She gave the baby a long bath, carefully and lovingly, all the while talking to the infant as if it understood what she was saying.

She lay with the baby tightly, and unhealthily, held in her arms all night, hardly daring to move in case she woke it. She would joyfully jump up to change her and make a feed for her when she demanded it. She danced through the house in sheer enjoyment.

The next morning, Thursday, she wrapped the baby warmly and headed for her favourite spot, on a crowded beach, where she sat under a rented umbrella on a blanket in the soft, white sand singing silly songs to a mostly sleeping little girl. Passersby lingered to join in her happiness and old ladies stopped to admire the baby, happy for Jeanie, who nodded when asked 'first one, is it?'

Tired, happy and in another world, Jeanie climbed the steep steps up to the car park in the heat of the afternoon.

Her plan was to head straight back to the holiday cottage to give the baby another leisurely bath, feed her and put her down to sleep. Jeanie, herself, needed a bath.

As she came out of the car park her heart almost stopped. A policeman with a dog came walking towards her. She stood still, cold with guilt, hardly breathing.

## Chapter 36

The policeman strolled past Jeanie, ignoring her completely.

She climbed into the driver's seat and sat for a moment with eyes closed, baby resting on the steering wheel, until her heartbeat slowed down. Then she started up the car and drove slowly out of the parking lot.

Realising that she had hardly eaten for two days and feeling very hungry, Jeanie prepared a thick sandwich for herself after she had put the baby to bed at about 7 that evening. With a contented sigh, her shock of the afternoon hidden, she unsuspectingly settled down to watch television, a steaming cup of coffee in her hand. Not a thought for the outcome of her actions or the unsure future crossed her mind.

The shock came with the regional news.

Looking straight into Jeanie's face, the newsreader reported that 'A two-day old baby girl was abducted from the female non-white wing of Valkenberg hospital sometime during this afternoon. The police are asking anyone who was visiting the hospital during the day to please telephone Caledon Square, or the local police station,' with both telephone numbers appearing on the screen.

Jeanie went into a cold sweat. She had expected that ...what had she expected? She could not say. She had, she supposed, hoped that Zogi would hold the front and refuse the adoption. But how would Zogi explain the missing baby? Well, it was her baby, wasn't it? And she had the right to ask Jeanie to look after the baby, didn't she?

Panic made her confused and unreasonable. She paced up and down in the little sitting room. Then, checking that the baby was where she had left her in the middle of the big double bed in the bedroom, Jeanie walked out onto the verandah of the cottage and stood staring at the moving waves in the distance.

A sudden wind came up and she heard it howling in the distance, sweeping down from the mountains at Muizenberg, down across the houses. Strandfontein was still very undeveloped and the sand dunes moved, almost overnight sometimes, as the strong winds swept across the beach across the few tiny houses built along the boulevard which ran parallel to the beach.

The house of the Pillays was two streets off the main street and Jeanie caught a glimpse of the disturbed sea through the gap between the two houses on the other side of the road. She felt unsettled and cold, so she went inside and sat in the dark room, television switched off and no sound but the howling wind and the occasional bark of a dog in the distance breaking into her tumultuous mind.

Zogi had obviously said nothing, and it was being treated as a normal abduction. She felt alarm, but also a complacency. Deep down she believed that they would never think of her as an abductor. She could not see them connecting her with the abduction.

Jeanie fell into a light sleep in the dark room and was awoken by a loud knock on the door. She sprang up, disturbed and sweating even before she had decided what to do. She did not want to open the door thinking that if she stayed quiet, the person might go away, knowing that Mrs. Pillay was not there.

The banging continued. She was too frozen to move.

The noise woke the baby up and she started screaming at the top of her voice. This confused Jeanie completely. She ran into the bedroom, grabbed the baby and held her tight, hoping that the screams would subside.

The baby cried louder, for by now the person on the doorstep shouted through the loudly, 'Nurse Dean, open up. It's the police! Open up, please!' There was nothing else to do but to go to the front door and face them.

## Chapter 37

She recognised Van der Merwe. Bile rose up in her throat with the memory of his taunting in detention.

'Got you this time,' he said with a satisfied smile. 'Not only a commie but a criminal commie, ey!'

The black policeman who was standing behind Van der Merwe came forward and tried to take the baby out of Jeanie's arms. An incredible strength flashed through Jeanie's system. She clung to the baby and held onto it with all her strength. The baby stopped screaming abruptly.

'You'll kill the child,' the policeman said, trying to pull her arms away from the baby. He tugged at her arms. Then Van der Merwe stepped up behind her and put his strong arm around her neck, bending her over backwards. She was forced to let go and the baby almost dropped to the floor before the other policeman managed to grab hold of her and walked away to the police car parked outside the house.

Jeanie watched him as if in a dream. Her control snapped. She screamed.

'You stinking, rotten bastards!' Jeanie shouted.

She stopped abruptly as she saw Van der Merwe's big paw of a hand come up. A memory of backhanded slaps across her face stopped her.

'Go and put on something decent. You are coming with us!' Van der Merwe said, leering down onto her breasts which were bulging up out of Zogi's skimpy, low-knecked cotton top, two sizes too small for her.

Quietly Jeanie turned around, followed by Van der Merwe, whose bulk cast a menacing shadow over her as she walked down the passage to the bedroom. She turned to close the door behind her.

'Oh, no, you don't,' the man said as he stood in the door. 'Just get dressed. I want to see what you are up to. I don't trust you junkies.' She looked up at him with pure hatred in her eyes. He laughed and said, 'I know all about your junkie friend. The long eyes of the law, hey,' he jeered.

She turned her back to him, threw on a big skirt over the pyjama bottoms she was still wearing. She found a cardigan on the back of the wicker chair which stood in the corner of the room and turned around to face her future with uncombed, fuzzy dry hair in a tight halo around her head.

Van der Merwe followed closely behind Jeanie and held out his hand for the key after she had locked the door. 'You're also going to be done for unlawful entry,' he said spitefully as he put the key into his pocket.

It was not too long ago that Jeanie had travelled in a police car. Going through the streets where Jeanie knew she might be recognised, she turned her head down. The baby was in the other car with the black policeman.

What were they going to do with her? Who will look after her tonight? Perhaps they will let her go back to the hospital, back to Zogi. But then, Zogi might by now have been discharged from hospital. They would not give the baby to her because the adoptive parents surely must have the right to take the baby back with them. Or perhaps – hope against hope - Zogi had after all not signed the adoption papers.

And what the hell was Van der Merwe doing with the uniformed branch? He was a security cop. He had grabbed at the opportunity to be the one to take her into custody, just to get the satisfaction of insulting her further, this she knew.

Strangely, Jeanie was not very afraid. Just ashamed as she sat in the back of the racing police car with her head down. She had been in detention too many times to worry too much about spending another night in a police cell. At least, this time, she was not going to be held under the restrictive detention laws, but had the less isolative rights of an ordinary prisoner. That consoled her and she did not show any fear as she caught Van der Merwe's eye in the rear-view mirror when she lifted her head.

Whereas she did not feel fear, her shame increased as she was marched through the charge office where other people were sitting waiting, hoping she would not be recognised while she stood back as Van der Merwe punched in security numbers to open the door into the interview rooms behind the front desk. She was taken into a holding room with about ten other women, most of them drunk. She was left there.

She sat in a corner, happy that she was not recognised by any of the other women. She did not want to speak with any of them and they left her alone. That is, she did not speak to any of them until the early hours of the next morning.

An elderly black woman, over seventy years of age, was roughly pushed through the iron gate in the early hours of the next morning. She walked across the room and lowered her heavy body down onto the floor in the corner next to Jeanie. The woman pulled her skirt down over her legs and sat with her head leaning against the wall. Jeanie thought her eyes were closed, although she could not be sure in the dark. After about fifteen minutes, Jeanie could hear her heavy breathing and her head dropped sideways, onto Jeanie's shoulder.

Jeanie was uncomfortable. The bit of blanket she had been sitting on had moved out from under her and she could feel the coldness of the bare cement floor creeping up into her bottom. She did not want to move as she was reluctant to wake up the poor old woman, who had looked so drawn and tired in that brief moment when the harsh electric light had been switched on while she was pushed into the cell.

The woman was snoring softly, her clean, warm breath blowing straight onto Jeanie's cheek. Jeanie sat trying to keep still, awkwardly moving her bottom so as to squeeze onto a bit more of the blanket, which was being shared by at least six women on her side of the room.

Her movement woke the old lady up. She sat upright and said something. It sounded like Zulu to Jeanie, who did not understand any African language.

'I'm sorry, but I can't speak Zulu,' she said shyly.

The woman brought her face forward in the dark, her long, regal nose almost touching Jeanie's. 'Ow, you Capetonians!' she said, shaking her head. 'You should be ashamed that you cannot speak the language of your forefathers!'

Jeanie felt ashamed. Ashamed, not because she could not speak the language of her ancestors, but ashamed that she had not bothered to learn any African language, having always been separated, by colour, education and class from the Xhosa in Cape Town.

'Sorry, ma,' she said respectfully. The old lady laughed and said in perfect English, 'It's alright, my girl. It is not our fault that we do not live the same lives. Perhaps you will do an old lady a favour. Send your children to learn the language of the land. Don't let them grow up not knowing each other, like the two of us.'

'Of course I will,' Jeanie whispered into the night.

'Oh, I'm so tired,' continued the woman after a brief silence. 'These horrible laws. Do you see all these girls? I'm quite sure that not half of them are criminals. Many of them are in here because of circumstances, like that one,' pointing to a petite, loud mouthed girl in a micro mini-skirt. 'The rest of them are here for doing absolutely nothing, like me.'

'You here under the pass laws?' asked Jeanie, who knew very little about the pass laws for, with an identity document identifying her as Coloured, she was by law exempt from carrying a pass. Jeanie's self-esteem had sunk quite quickly as the woman spoke, for she thought that the woman regarded her as one of the few criminals here.

'Not this time. And I'm not yet expected to carry a pass, thank God. It's our men who have to carry them' came the reply. This Jeanie did not know. The old lady could see her puzzled look and continued. 'You should know the law, my girl,' a smile in her voice. 'Black women don't live in cities unless we are servants!' referring to the Native (Black) Urban Areas Act against which white women like Helen Suzman and the English woman Helen Joseph raised their loud political voices in the all white parliament.

'No. This time it is because they don't want me to make money for my grandchildren to go to school.'

Jeanie sat quietly, listening, not quite understanding. 'They say I run a shebeen,' the old lady said softly, now more seriously. 'What's wrong with brewing the drinks my mother and grandmother taught me to make for our men when they come home from a long day in the fields?' she asked reasonably, not questioning the illegality of selling it in defiance of the liquor laws.

Jeanie agreed, for honest need comes before the law when your family is suffering, and your grandchildren cannot go to school because there is no money for school fees. In both their minds there could be no criminal intent when the white children, whose parents have the money, and the coloured children who have the privilege, do not have to pay to attend school. Good for you, ma! Jeanie thought, and she knew that the old lady was grateful for her supportive silence.

'I've been picked up so many times, I've stopped counting,' the old lady continued under her breath, speaking as if Jeanie was not there. 'The problem is, I don't have the right to live in Cape Town. I should be in the Transkei. But my daughter lives here in Guguletu. How can I survive there, so far away from them? So, they can go on picking me up for as many times as they like. If you get in, you must get out, hey?' she said, this time with laughter in her voice, turning her face to Jeanie.

This little conversation cheered Jeanie up. Suddenly she no longer felt quite so removed from the women around her. Most of us are here because of circumstances, she thought as she heard the woman's voice, and this comforted her.

She slept fitfully, sitting up with the old lady leaning heavily into her. As the night turned light, Jeanie heard snippets of low conversations between the women. She marvelled at the fact that not one of them asked questions or passed any opinions or judgment on each other.

At about six the morning she woke up properly, feeling tired, but determined to keep her faith strong.

They stood for two hours in the drafty corridor in the basement of the building, waiting to be checked out. They could see, at the end of the corridor, a bench with two uniformed officers sitting down and two standing beside the desk, as each woman's name was called, and her charge read to her.

Some coffee was passed along, black and bitter, with dry brown bread, cut in thick, unattractive slices. Jeanie refused to have any. Her stomach would not allow her to eat anything. The endless waiting had started up her fear again and she caught herself clenching her teeth. She forced her shoulders to relax and breathed deeply when the nerves in her diaphragm shivered as if mice were gnawing away at the tension inside her.

Jeanie's turn came, and she was read the charge of Kidnapping and Abduction of a New Born Baby. She stood without any expression on her face, listening, resigned to her fate. The night had shown her that being with other women was not such a bad experience and that she would just take things as they came. Her big worry was her job and the consequences her actions would have on her future.

Right now, she needed a toilet, so every other need was pushed aside.

The policewoman who was standing by the turnstile which led through to the back door looked up when Jeanie said, in her quiet, polite voice, 'I need to go to the toilet, please.' The woman stared at Jeanie for a moment as if she were considering a most unusual request. Then she nodded at a young policewoman who was standing against the wall behind Jeanie, who stepped forward, grabbed Jeanie by the arm, and marched her through a door in the short passage. She swung the door open and stood in the doorway, pointing. Jeanie walked through into a small back room without a door and a toilet seat facing out.

She was grateful for her long skirt as she sat down, facing the policewoman who was watching her all the time. Using the toilet paper afterwards was the embarrassing part, but she got through it. She had hardly stood up when the woman stood aside for her to pass back into the passage. There was no tap in sight for hand washing, so Jeanie merely rubbed her hands against her thighs as she walked out to join the queue in the short passage.

They were bundled into a huge police truck and arrived at the courthouse about an hour later. Once again, they were delivered straight into the bowels of the building. In the basement they were pushed along like sheep, behind big chicken wire fences, to await their turn to be called into court.

The three hours wait before she was called undid whatever confidence she had built up during the night. When her turn came, Jeanie was feeling really scared and felt the panic rise up in her throat, burning up through her gut and settling in the back of her throat with a sour taste. Her mouth smelt. She had not spoken to anyone except for the brief few words she had said to the old lady the night before. She felt dirty.

She was led up the narrow steps into the court room where, this time, it was her turn to face the magistrate. Perhaps I am being punished for what I did to Gregory, she thought as she stood there, listening to the prosecutor reading out the charge against her. Other than to confirm her name, she was not asked any other questions.

She stood half dazed, trying to understand the proceedings. A conversation was being carried on between the magistrate and the prosecutor, which she could hear only a few snatches of.

'Mrs. Dean,' said the magistrate after a few minutes, addressing her for the first time, 'the State is prepared to let you out on bail of 500 Rand. Unless you pay this money, you will have to remain in custody until you appear at the Supreme Court next week. On the charge of abduction. Do you understand?'

'Yes,' was all she could say, not sure whether she had enough money in her bank account.

'You may go and sit down,' the magistrate said with a nod, at the same time closing the file and putting his papers on the side of the bench, reaching for another folder.

As she was about to sit down next to the prosecutor's desk, not knowing what was to happen next and his ignoring her completely, she saw a policeman at the top of the steps which led down to the basement. He beckoned to her. She turned around and dutifully walked towards him, not knowing what was going to happen, wondering how she was to get hold of 500 Rands.

Jeanie followed the policeman, who turned around and walked down the steps when she reached him. When they got downstairs, she was taken to a room for fingerprinting. The policewoman there slowly and painstakingly took first the one, then the other thumb, pushed each one onto an ink pad, and pushed them onto a blank sheet of paper in the folder in front of her.

She said not a word to Jeanie. Not bothering to take one of the bits of paper which were lying around on the desk, Jeanie nervously wiped the black ink from her fingers onto her skirt.

When the woman said, 'OK, next one,' Jeanie clumsily stepped aside, not knowing what to do. She just continued to stand there, feeling silly and lost, not knowing the rights of the criminally accused.

Then she realised one thing she did know. Each accused person had the right to a lawyer. Catching the eye of the big policeman who was standing beside the little table, overseeing the finger printing, she approached him and asked to use the telephone. He pointed to a public phone which was on the wall not far from where he stood.

'I've got no money on me,' Jeanie said to him, boldly. He shrugged and looked the other way, and she went to stand with her back to the wall, wondering how one insists on a right given by law, when the law does not tell one how to get to that right.

Then she remembered that one could still make reverse charge calls and the light appeared again in her bleak predicament. She went back to the phone on the wall, which hung as unused as the single chair which stood next to it. She dialled the free phone number for telephone enquiries and was given her lawyer's number. Luckily Jeanie had a good memory for numbers, and she phoned her lawyer's office.

'Oh, Mrs. Dean,' the secretary who answered the telephone said. 'Mr. Ahmed is consulting at the moment, but

I'm sure he would want to speak with you,' she said. Jeanie wondered why they accepted a reverse charge call from her and secondly why her very busy lawyer would interrupt his other business to speak to her, but she was to know immediately he came through on the line.

'Hello Jeanie. You're famous, hey,'

'Hello Kariem,' she answered, wondering what he was talking about.

'It's all over the papers, Jeanie,' he continued. This made her come out in a cold sweat. Up to then she had not given a thought to the effect of her actions on her public self.

'Oh Lord!' was all she could say.

'Where are you, Jeanie? I'd hoped you would call me before going to court.' 'I never thought of it,' Jeanie mumbled softly. She really had not thought of asking him to come to court, until that moment.

'It's too late now,' she continued. 'I was in there for only a few moments, anyway.'

'Where are you now, Jeanie?' he asked.

'I'm still at Wynberg Magistrate's Court.'

'Did they give you bail?'

'Yes, 500 Rands,' she said, hoping.

'Got the money?' Of course, he would ask that.

'No,' she replied, her heart racing, her mind urging her to ask him to help her. But she did not. Despite her predicament, Jeanie Dean could not surmount her pride.

'Is there anybody I can phone to ask for the money for you, Jeanie?' he asked.

Jeanie remained silent for a while, thinking. Not one person of those she knew would help her with money. The only person whom she could have asked would have been Zogi, but that was impossible.

'What about your husband, Gregory?' her divorce lawyer asked her, and Jeanie took in a deep breath of frustration.

'I don't think so,' said Jeanie, trying to keep the repugnance out of her voice. What is the man thinking about.

'When are you appearing in court again?' he asked. Jeanie told him, and the only help she could get from him was, 'I'll try my best to do something for you. If I don't then we will see each other sometime tomorrow. I will arrange a visit at the police cells.'

When she put the telephone down, Jeanie realised, for the first time since she had been taken to the police station the night before, the depth of the pickle she was in. Her shoulders sagged and her feet dragged as she slowly walked back to stand against the cold wall.

## Chapter 38

The big clock high against the wall was ticking forward painfully slowly. Jeanie watched it intently in her effort to keep her mind off the mess she was in. She wondered what she would be doing at 3.30 tomorrow morning, or the morning thereafter. The prospect of spending such a long time incarcerated was frightening.

Her mind kept going back to the baby. She thought of the feel of the baby's soft skin against her cheek. She thought of the down on her tiny arms and on her back; the way she suckled at everything which touched her lips; her wizened frown when she cried; her vulnerability. Jeanie's eyes clouded over with tears, and she looked back up at the clock to take her mind off the deep distress inside her. It had moved only two minutes.

Someone called her name, in that flat way that names are impersonalised when coming from the bored mouths of people who hate their jobs.

Jeanie stood up and turned her head towards the direction of the sound. She put her hand up like a little schoolgirl, too afraid to use her voice, which, she suspected, would have let her down.

A policewoman was approaching her, accompanied by a plump white woman. The woman's grey hair was sending off sparkles as she moved along the corridor under the bare electric bulb, the softness of her recent blue rinse matching the colour of her suit, the grey so often favoured by those over sixty.

The policewoman strode out in front of the woman and confronted Jeanie with an air of satisfaction on her ugly, scarred face, which sat on a thin neck. 'Your head office telephoned. They want you to hand your car back immediately,' without introduction or greeting.

Jeanie took the long, brown, official envelope which the woman held out to her. Still looking at the policewoman's face, Jeanie pulled out the sheet of paper from the envelope which someone had either not bothered to seal, or which had been opened.

Her eyes ran down the short letter and came to rest on the middle paragraph, the words burning into her mind as she read:

It is with regret that I have to advise you of the decision by the Board of Governors taken at the aforesaid meeting, that your services as a District Midwife with the Cape Provincial Administration is to be, and is hereby, suspended with immediate effect, pending determination of the aforementioned disciplinary proceedings by the South African Nursing and Midwifery Council. All equipment in your possession needs to be returned within two weeks of receipt of this letter, to our Head Offices at 540 St George's Street. Kindly hand over the keys to motor vehicle Ford Anglia Registration Number 1902 GOV to the bearer of this letter, who will acknowledge receipt in writing.

'Well?' asked the woman, a screen of professionalism hiding whatever personality she had.

Jeanie raised her head and wearily shrugged, not able to voice the extreme emotion she was at that moment feeling, too shocked to know what to say. 'You've got to give us the car keys, Mrs. Dean. Where is the car?'

Jeanie looked at the woman who was standing behind the policewoman, a silent witness to the erosion of her life. She had not said a word to either the woman or the policewoman now standing facing her, waiting for a response. Catching Jeanie's eye, the woman turned to the policewoman and said, 'Let me speak to Mrs. Dean for a moment.'

'You cannot do this where we cannot see you,' came the reply.

The woman merely turned her back to the policewoman and faced Jeanie who was still standing with her back to the wall. She shifted the folders she was holding in her right hand under her left arm and, offering her hand to Jeanie, said 'I'm Zogi's social worker,' in a heavy Afrikaans accent.

Jeanie's listless handshake was returned with a firm, warm, strong grasp. 'Oh,' was all Jeanie could say.

'Zogi sent for me and asked me to find out what your bail conditions were, after the report in the papers about the hearing this morning' continued the woman. She was still holding Jeanie's hand tightly, smiling kindly at her.

'Perhaps you would allow me to suggest something?' asked the woman, as Jeanie had still not said a word.

Jeanie nodded mutely and the woman continued, 'We need to talk somewhere. Perhaps you would come with me. I will tell the police that I'll have the car delivered to them later this evening. Is that alright with you?' Only too glad to let go of the decision, in fact, not having the slightest idea of where the car keys might be, Jeanie nodded. 'Yes, please,' the first words she said to the woman. She stood quietly for about five minutes, watching the grey-haired woman go over to the policewoman, who nodded her agreement.

'Come on,' said the lady when she returned to Jeanie, 'I paid the bail before I came downstairs. Let's get out of here.'

Jeanie's heart lifted. The thought of getting out of the depressing building made her feel lighter and, together, they walked to the door at the bottom of the steps, waited for it to be unlocked, and up the wide, dark stairway to the ground floor, where they had to stop again while the policeman sorted out the papers. He read Jeanie's bail conditions to her and handed her the paper, unlocked the outer door, and Jeanie walked into another shock in the strong Cape mid-afternoon sunshine.

The woman next to her was just saying, 'My name is Valerie Koen,' as the double doors swung to behind them, when a young woman came up to them. She wore a beige trench coat under which Jeanie glimpsed a black skirt and calf-length boots. She smiled at Jeanie and, politely, Jeanie returned a weak smile to her.

All expectations of friendliness were shattered immediately when the woman said to Jeanie, 'I'm a reporter with the Cape Herald. You abducted a baby Mrs. Dean. Isn't that the cruellest thing a midwife could do?' Jeanie froze, unable to believe her ears.

Then she saw the others behind the woman.

She tried to cover her face with her hands as her eyes were blinded by bulbs flashing. God, thought Jeanie, the entire South Africa is to see me like this: hair thick and uncombed, skirt soiled, long crumbled shirt, with a cardigan now full of the black marks of shame.

About four people were approaching her and Mrs. Koen. Two of them, an overpoweringly tall, thin man and a serious, business-like woman, pushed past the first reporter, up the steps, ahead of the others, and Jeanie caught the green, greedy eyes of the predatory journalist.

He opened his mouth and started, 'Mrs. Dean –' when Jeanie swung around with the speed of a hunted animal. She bumped her head into the swing doors and, pushing Mrs. Koen out of the way, not bothering to hold the doors back for the woman, Jeanie ran through, back into the passage. Questions were raining onto her from behind, 'Have you got anything to say,' 'I believe you are not living with your husband-'

She came to a standstill in the quietness of the passage, bewildered, but appreciating the quietness and safety of the court building, when, 'Kom sit hier, my kind' (Come sit here, my child) Mrs. Koen's low voice accompanied a soft touch on her arm, pushing her gently down onto a bench against the wall. Jeanie almost collapsed onto the seat, and Mrs. Koen sat herself down next to Jeanie.

'They cannot come into the court building,' she said with authority.

Jeanie was shocked. Shivering, she allowed Mrs. Koen's warm palms to cover her hands while the woman sat patiently waiting for Jeanie to stop trembling. Mrs. Koen did not say anything for a long while, waiting for Jeanie to look up at her.

Eventually Jeanie felt the tremors slowly subside. Her feet were feeling like blocks of ice and her face was clammy.

'Oh god, Mrs. Koen,' she whispered, biting on her bottom lip, 'it's much worse than I thought.'

The woman nodded thoughtfully, watching Jeanie intently. She was silent for a moment, then said quietly, '…Think we can go now? My car is parked at the back of the building. I'll ask them if I can pull it into the basement, then we can leave straight into a back street.' Jeanie nodded her appreciation.

They did manage to avoid the reporters by taking the back entrance. While Jeanie waited inside the building, Mrs. Koen fetched the car, and they were allowed out of a small side gate.

They were both quiet as Valerie Koen carefully drove along the Upper Main Road towards Claremont. Jeanie's mind sat heavily in her head, like a cold stone. The realisation that she now had no job was the final straw. Her work, her emotional shield, had protected her throughout her life, especially lately. Now it had crumbled, and

Jeanie felt exposed, her mind refusing to see past the cloud of distress surrounding her into the unforeseen, dark future. Her job, her only lifeline, had been wrenched away from her.

Jeanie sank her head onto her chest in the car and sobbed silently while Mrs. Koen drove along slowly, giving the woman the quiet space she needed to give vent to the emotions which imploded inside her.

Jeanie cried quietly but with such force inside her tiny chest, that the blood vessels in her neck and on her forehead stood out against the pressure behind them. She kept her face turned away from Mrs. Koen, so that the woman would not see her tears. They rolled down her cheeks, unchecked, as she fixedly stared out of the car window. Through her tears she saw the blue of the sky turn into storm clouds, and it looked as if they engulfed the car which seemed to be travelling right into their thundering bowels. As if echoing Jeanie's sadness, rain drops started falling onto the windscreen.

Her mind turned to the baby.

Jeanie could not wait any longer, and sounded quite frightened when she said to Mrs. Koen, 'Do you know where the baby is? Is she safe? Who is she with?'

The lady took her eyes off the road for a moment to give Jeanie one of her understanding smiles. 'Yes,' she said. 'The baby is safe and happy. I placed her with a woman in Crawford last night. I know the woman, she has fostered many children needing care.'

Jeanie wanted to know more, also about Zogi and what she had said, but did not ask any more questions.

When Mrs. Koen said, 'I thought the best thing for us to do is to go to my place,' Jeanie was surprised. 'You can then phone your lawyer from there and he can decide, after you've had a bath and a little sleep, what to do next. How does that sound to you?'

This Jeanie had not expected. Mrs. Koen was Zogi's social worker and Jeanie knew that it was unusual for a social worker to do all that, and then to take the risk of offering Jeanie a place to stay.

That was, until the woman said, quite matter of factly, 'Jeanie, I am not only Zogi's social worker. I am also your comrade,' and this surprised Jeanie even more. It should not have done, for in the underground one did not often know who was doing what or even if they were doing anything or nothing, for the less you knew about each other, the better it was for everyone.

Looking at her quietly from the side, Jeanie tried to place the woman, searching her brain for clues as to where she might have seen her before, but she could not remember. It was enough for her right now to know that Mrs. Koen was on her side.

## Chapter 39

It had been the night of the rally in Johannesburg! A light suddenly came on in her brain as she looked at Valerie's silhouette reflecting against the side window.

That day when they had all been so excited, for the underground movement had hired buses to take the women to the Soweto stadium for a celebration of August 9, South African Women's day.

Then, in the bus, a white woman, the other white woman of two in their bus from Cape Town, had stood up and the singing stopped.

'The police have heard of our meeting in Jo'burg,' she said aloud, and all the women went quiet. Jeanie, who had been sitting in the seat facing Valerie, even then had admired the woman. An Afrikaner, a social worker, who had committed her life to the struggle long before Jeanie had known of the struggles of her own people.

'So, we are re-routing to Durban!' she shouted into the confusion and celebration.

No magistrate could stop the strength of the underground when it moved! Not having had the luxury of telegrams or telephones, the liberation struggle had pushed and planned for exactly such occasions. Messages passed smoothly on foot, in cars, by bus and train, from street to street to the next town and villages. Across the land street committees passed messages which were delivered mouth to mouth, in notes scrambled and copied, passed on and scattered in orderly relays, and delivered within a day. Tapped phones, fax machines and telegrams had never been able to stop bush communication when it had to happen.

Within 24 hours all the buses and cars had been rerouted and the shops and cafés at large service stations along the route to Johannesburg, owned by white informants and their cronies, had to get rid of tons of food which they had stacked up to sell to the thousands whom they had heard – tipped off by boasting policemen – were en route to a rally in Johannesburg.

That weekend stood out in Jeanie's mind for the rest of her days. The joy, the hugging, the dissipation of fear, which comeradie brings had carried her through many a lonely dark night.

And Valerie Koen, her comrade, had come here to rescue her!

Valerie smiled into the windscreen, as from the side of her eye she caught Jeanie's expression. 'Remember Johan, my brother?' she asked, and Jeanie could not believe what her mind had been shouting at her all these long, long months.

Of course! It was Johan! The Afrikaner who had not been far from her mind all the time. Now she recognised that smile, an older face now covered in a beard, but with the same smiling eyes.

'I saw him at the court this afternoon,' Jeanie mumbled in amazement and Valerie laughed.

'Yes. He had spoken about you, Jeanie. He thought that you were shunning him.'

'Does he work at the court?'

'Yes, he is a defence lawyer. Does mostly political trials. Today he was there because he knew you would be there. We all read what had happened in the papers, and decided to come along to support you.' Unbelievable!

Valerie drew the car into a side street and turned to Jeanie.

'We have spoken with Zogi, Jeanie, and she has agreed.'

'Agreed?'

'Yes. Johan has spoken with her and told her her rights. The baby has to be at least six weeks old before a decision for adoption can become legal. As the court has not made an order of adoption, the baby is still Zogi's.'

Jeanie went completely still. This was beyond belief. She sat staring ahead, not moving a muscle, too surprised to know what to say.

'So Johan is, right now, addressing the Judge in chambers, and the case against you will be withdrawn.'

'What about Kariem, my lawyer. Why did he not say this to me?' Jeanie blurted out as her anger surfaced.

'You have the right to sack him as your lawyer. What were you doing anyway, going to that verkrampte (conservative) government stooge?' and Jeanie breathed her first normal breath in days.

And so it was. Jeanie did not need to go back into court again.

The next time she was to see Johan, he carried the baby in his arms and tenderly placed it into Jeanie's.

She looked up into those serious, soft green eyes with their familiar laughter lines as he reached for her head above the baby and nestled it against his cheek, as the baby slept quietly into its warm, protective future.

Table of Contents

Chapter 1; *11*
Chapter 2; *29*
Chapter 3; *37*
Chapter 4; *41*
Chapter 5; *51*
Chapter 6; *61*
Chapter 7; *67*
Chapter 8; *73*
Chapter 9; *75*
Chapter 10; *83*

Chapter 11; *87*
Chapter 12; *95*
Chapter 13; *99*
Chapter 14; *105*
Chapter 15; *115*
Chapter 16; *119*
Chapter 17; *123*
Chapter 18; *127*
Chapter 19; *133*
Chapter 20; *139*

Chapter 21; *145*
Chapter 22; *153*
Chapter 23; *161*
Chapter 24; *173*
Chapter 25; *179*
Chapter 26; *183*
Chapter 27; *189*
Chapter 28; *193*
Chapter 29; *195*
Chapter 30; *201*

Chapter 31; *215*
Chapter 32; *225*
Chapter 33; *233*
Chapter 34; *243*
Chapter 35; *255*
Chapter 36; *261*
Chapter 37; *265*
Chapter 38; *279*
Chapter 39; *287*

europe books